RUNNING WITCH

A SEASHELL COVE PARANORMAL MYSTERY
BOOK 4

T. THORN COYLE

1

August in Seashell Cove was maximum tourist-town. The sidewalks outside the plate glass shop windows teemed with tourists wearing shorts and Seashell Cove sweatshirts. People always think *beach* equals *hot*, but on the Oregon Coast? You just never know. Sure, there's the occasional freak heat dome, but mostly? Highs are in the low seventies, and sixty degrees with wind off the Pacific. If you aren't used to it, that can feel a lot cooler than sixty degrees inland.

While navigating crowded sidewalks wasn't my favorite thing, I appreciated the tourist crush when I was inside the bookshop, like today. Even Rhiannon was on her best behavior and working as hard as a shop cat could. She was currently showing off in front of a stack of summer reads in the front window, preening at every person who slowed down to admire her glossy black fur and, consequently, look at the books on display.

Yeah. Tourists meant customers. Customers meant sales. Sales meant kibble and treats.

Tourist-customers also meant herding small children

with dripping ice cream cones away from the merchandise.

"I'm so sorry," I said to the exhausted-looking parent as I led the small family out the door. It opened onto our pocket-sized parking lot, which was not the most pleasant place to enjoy the sunny day, but better than getting chocolate all over the store.

The poor guy was at his wit's end, what with the ice-cream-eating toddler and a baby in a sling strapped to his front.

I held the door propped open, blocking the way back in. "I'll be happy to hold the books you were looking at until, erm..."

The toddler plopped herself down on the low wall between the shop entrance and our tiny parking lot and began happily smearing chocolate with sprinkles all over the front of her shirt. The rest of the ice cream covered her cherubic little face and her blond curls.

I refrained from tapping the "No Food or Drink Inside" sign next to the door.

The man sighed and rubbed the crease between his eyebrows.

"Thanks," he said. "I've got wet wipes and will make sure she's clean before we head back in."

Now it was his turn to sink onto the low wall.

"Bebe, the ice cream goes in your mouth."

I shut the door firmly behind me with a clatter of bells and leaned against it for a moment. I exhaled and wiped my hands down the front of my size sixteen jeans before pasting a smile on my face, straightening up, and heading back toward the counter, where my shop manager, Duncan, was busy ringing people up.

"Need any help?" I asked him. He glanced at me from

behind his heavy, black-framed glasses, smiled, and shook his head.

"I'm good. But while you were outside, I think I heard a minor crash." He jerked his bleached-blond head toward the back of the shop.

I stifled a groan. A crash could mean one of three things:

A - more toddlers, getting up to who knows what?

B - one of our more senior customers, who had bumped into something, dropped a book, or worst case scenario, fallen.

C - the resident ghost, trying to get my attention again.

Yeah. The Widening Gyre has its own ghost, name of Biff. Even now, I heard giggles, and headed toward the sound. Rounding the corner, just past the thrillers and mysteries aisle, I almost tripped over the gigglers. Three ghost-hunting preteens were taking selfies in front of the antique mirror my part-time workers—two marketing-savvy teenagers named Tabitha and Tracy—had engraved to read "The Widening Gyre" at the top, with the outline of a ghostly man peeking out of one corner.

Bookstagram was going to get another photo, hashtag HauntedBookshop.

I'd fought the whole "cash in on the ghost" idea, but what can I say? The teens were right. Biff brought in customers and sold merchandise, like the T-shirt I was wearing, that showed a cute cartoon ghost carrying a stack of books.

Except Biff wasn't a cute cartoon ghost. He was the mostly genial former proprietor of the bookshop that had once been my father's, and was now mine all mine, shaky finances and all. Though I had to admit, the teens' social media and merch ideas were helping with the finances. A lot. It even paid their wages.

I gave the ghost hunters a thumbs-up and continued toward the back of the shop, pausing to reshelve some books along the way. I stopped to help an older gentleman find the latest Bernard Cornwall seafaring yarn and finally made it back to the place Tabitha and Tracy had started calling Biff's Corner: the paranormal and occult section where Biff like to hang out. I was never sure if that was Biff's idea of a joke or not. You know, ghosts hanging out with the ghost books? Maybe I'm the only one who finds that amusing.

Sure enough, there was not one, but two books splayed out on the floor near the comfy chair set in the corner under a good reading light.

"Dang it, Biff," I muttered, "why are you throwing books again? We've talked about this."

I looked around but didn't see the former proprietor hovering anywhere. And it didn't feel cold or anything, like it usually did when Biff was around. I heard a small noise. Was that a sob? Or was it a hamster coughing? I looked again. Nope. Still didn't see anyone.

"Biff?" My voice was less certain this time.

And there it came again. A weird sob followed by a definite sniff. My head whipped from side to side. Still nothing. Only books, a photo of Biff in the store way back sometime in the 1990s, the comfy chair and reading lamp.

Wait a minute.

There, on the top of the low bookcase near the chair was a statue I didn't recognize. A small, gray stone lump with big ears and wings. Had one of the teens left it? They picked things up at yard sales sometimes and brought them in as decorations. But they were supposed to run everything by me.

I stepped closer, peering at the shelf above the Haunted Oregon section. There was a small, gray stone gargoyle with a bow on its head.

A stone bow, you know, not a pink party bow. But still. *Sniff.*

I stifled a groan. This was just what I needed. A distraught gargoyle.

"What's wrong?"

The gargoyle froze, one stone tear leaking out of its right stone eye. It didn't say a word. Didn't sob. Didn't sniff.

"You can pretend you're just a stone gargoyle, an inanimate object made by a human, if you really want to," I said, looking around again, keeping my voice low. "But I know that's not true. So you may as well tell me what you're doing here and what's wrong."

The gargoyle gasped, and then disappeared with a *pop.* What the heck? Gargoyles could appear and disappear? Was there some kind of alternate dimension in the back corner of my store? Or was this a creatures-made-of-stone thing?

Or had the gargoyle been taking lessons from my Uncle Cyrus, the warlock? One of Cyrus's most annoying traits was his ability to pop in and out of places at will. And yeah, being a witch who didn't have that ability? I was probably a little jealous.

Well, there were two ways to find out what powers gargoyles have: either the stone creature would appear again so I could ask it, or I'd have to set Tracy and Tabitha onto research duty again.

Luckily, the teens enjoyed the task. As a matter of fact, they should have been in for their shift by now.

I sighed and bent to pick up the fallen books, smoothing the rumpled pages. Thankfully, they were both used, and not valuable except for the information inside. The first was on Scottish castles—I guess that made sense for a gargoyle—and the second was on the care and feeding of your new puppy.

What was that book even doing back in this section? Animal books were down a different aisle. Shaking my head, I slotted the Scottish castle book into the architecture section, which was at least just across the aisle, and then went to find a home for the puppy book.

Which reminded me, Stefon was supposed to be meeting me soon so we could go for our regular jog. I'd been slacking a bit lately because it wasn't as much fun jogging along the beach during tourist season, but a witch has to keep fit, you know? Besides, I had signed us both up for the Wag a Lot Fun Run that benefited the local animal shelter. There was a 1K Puppy Run, a 5K Regular People run, and then a 10K for more serious runners.

5K was pretty easy for me, but was I really up for 10K? Not at the rate I wasn't training.

The bells on the front door rang again. I headed up the central aisle, straightening shelves as I went, and there he was: my big, beautiful, dark knight. Literally. Stefon was a computer whiz, a D&D geek, and a belted knight of the Society for Medieval Anachronism, or SMA, and his skin was smooth as brown silk.

My skin? It took a lot of unguents to look this good when you were pasty pale like me.

"Hey babe." He smiled his luscious smile, close-cut dark beard curling up around his lips. Today's uniform was black jeans and his favorite *Sisko is My Captain* T-shirt. The shirt outlined his massive chest, shoulders, and belly in a way that made my mouth water. Give me a muscular keg over a six-pack any day.

I gave him a quick kiss.

He squeezed me, then looked around at the busy store, brow furrowing. "You gonna be able to take off for our run?"

I nodded. "As soon as Tabitha and Tracy show up, I'll be good to go. As long as we can stop by my place to change."

I looked down at my own jeans and T-shirt. Running in jeans was something I only did when being chased by a pissed-off centaur, and that wasn't high on my list of favorite things.

The bells on the door announced the entry of the dad, baby, and much cleaner toddler, followed by the two teenagers, here for their shift.

I grinned at all of them. "Welcome back to the Widening Gyre."

2

Stefon and I paced each other, skirting and dodging tourists foolishly clambering over what I call the fallen giants. These are trees washed to shore by the inevitable turning of the Pacific tides, leaving massive gray-brown carcasses on the sand.

Despite signs posted at every entrance cautioning people not to: climb the driftwood, make sculptures, disturb the wildlife, or *turn their backs on the ocean*...people did all of the above. All the time.

The result was a beach festooned with amazing driftwood sculptures and children balanced precariously on rocks and massive tree trunks. And at least two tourists are yanked to sea by sneaker waves every year. Seriously. The Oregon Coast does not mess around.

I regulated my breathing the way my barefoot running teacher showed me. Exhale, step two, three, four, exhale, step two, three, four. Breathing without consciously inhaling had felt strange at first, but once I got the hang of it, I'd taught it to Stefon, too. My lungs naturally filled on their own, and the result was much less huffing and puffing overall. Huh.

I was feeling pretty good, finding my stride. Maybe I *should* try for the 10K this year.

"Watch out!" A voice cracked across the happy seaside sounds. I stumbled into Stefon, who caught me just as an orange Frisbee sailed past, right where my head had been.

As I fell, my foot caught on a piece of driftwood and twisted. I stifled a yelp as Stefon gently lowered me to the sand.

"Hey! Sorry dude!" A blond man in his early twenties ran up, as did his dog, a golden retriever who excitedly sniffed around my injured ankle.

And then buried his nose in my crotch. Nice.

I shoved him away.

"Stop," blond dude said. "Hey, Board Wax! Knock it off. Leave the lady alone."

"Your dog's name is Board Wax?" I forgot my pain and annoyance for one second.

The guy grinned and smiled. "Yeah, pretty cool, huh? Beach dog."

I glanced at Stefon, who shrugged. What, did the guy think this was Malibu or something? I wanted to say *You're on the Oregon Coast, buddy. Get over yourself.*

But I needed to save my energy for dealing with my now throbbing ankle.

"Hey, man, I'm really sorry. My name is Carlson. Can I help you up?"

I groaned.

"I think I got it, man," Stefon replied, going into deal-with-the-strange-white-dude-in-board-shorts mode. He looked down at me, dark eyes flashing concern. "You ready to try, babe?"

"Now's as good a time as any," I said, though the thought of crawling up the steps that led up the steep incline, bridging the sand with the cliff tops, was daunting.

"I don't know if I can make it up the stairs," I said.

"Let's see if you can bear any weight first," Stefon said. Which was reasonable, coming from the person not in increasing pain.

Meanwhile, activity went on around us. Kites flying. Seagulls swooping. Children shrieking. And Carlson in his dumb shorts and sneakers, with Board Wax dancing around his ankles, clutching a battered orange Frisbee. He at least had the grace to look concerned.

"Okay," Stefon said, wrapping his big arms around me. I inhaled. He smelled like sweat and ocean, with a hint of amber. "Ready?"

"I guess."

"One. Two. Three." He hoisted me up, one hand beneath my armpit, my body smushed against his. I hopped on my good leg and then gingerly tried to place weight on my twisted right ankle.

If I was the cursing kind, well, let's just say some bleeped out words would have been happening.

"Ouch," I said. "No. No way."

"This is bad," Stefon said.

"How am I gonna make it up the steps?" I craned my neck to look up at the steep incline that rose three stories high.

"Babe," he said, brow creasing was worry, "I'm not sure. But we'll figure it out."

"Hey, Board Wax and I can help, dude."

Stefon shook his head. "I think you've done enough."

A look of hurt crossed Carlson's face.

"We didn't mean to…"

"I know," I interjected, staving off a long conversation I had no patience for. Seriously. The dude had hurt me, and I was trying to comfort him? "Really, I know. But look at me. And look at you."

Carlson was a skinny as a rail, and his happy, galumphing dog wasn't exactly reliable.

"Well," he said, eyes narrowing, "I see what you mean. But really, I'm strong. You know, all that surfing. As a matter of fact, I've got a boogie board in my car, we could use it as a sledge up the stairs!"

Stefon held out a hand, thank the Goddess, stopping Carlson from getting any more ideas.

"Thanks, man, but I think I've got it. Besides, I think Board Wax will get in the way."

"All right," said Carlson, face filled with disappointment. "Let's go, Board Wax, and leave these people alone."

Then unbelievably, he threw that dang Frisbee. Board Wax, golden tail flapping in the ocean breeze, chased after, leaping to grab it in his mouth.

"You're really throwing that Frisbee again?" Stefon shook his head.

Board Wax sped off with the orange disc in his slobbering mouth.

"Gotta run, dudes."

"You do that," I said to his back as he kicked up sand, chasing after the dog.

"Stefon. I think I need to rest. Can you set me down?"

He sighed. "I'm worried that if I let you sit and rest, your ankle will swell up more and we won't be able to get you out of here at all. Do you want me to call the paramedics?"

"No!" That was the last thing I needed. First, the

expense. And second, the embarrassment. "Don't you have any studly knight friends you can call?"

His face brightened. "Yeah. Great idea! Let's sit you down on this rock."

He angled me toward a boulder and eased me down. I groaned with relief. Moments later, I sat with my foot propped on a piece of driftwood, inhaling the ocean air as Stefon got out his phone and started texting.

A woman in a yellow head wrap and matching shorts walked over, dragging a small cooler and one child.

"I saw what happened," she said, brown face puckered with worry. "We have some ice left in the cooler. I was just about to leave so we won't be needing it anymore, and I've got a plastic baggie."

"Oh, that would be great," I said.

Stefon was pacing now, phone to his ear, talking urgently. The woman rummaged through the cooler as the toddler plunked its diapered butt onto the sand next to me and looked up and smiled. I smiled back.

"What's your name?" I asked.

"Cleo."

"Well, Cleo, I hope you had a good day at the beach."

The mother handed me a baggie full of ice wrapped in a paper towels.

"Thank you so much," I said, easing the ice onto my elevated ankle. "My name's Sarah, by the way."

"Not a problem. I'm Assata."

"Hey, does Cleo like books?"

"Books!" Cleo said.

The mother rolled her eyes but smiled.

"Cleo *loves* books. We're at the library every week, and she drags me into every bookstore we pass."

"Well," I said, "I've got the only bookshop in Seashell

Cove, and if you stop in today, tell my manager, Duncan—he's a white guy with black glasses—that Cleo can pick out any book she wants from the children's section."

Her face brightened. "Thank you! That'd be great! And better than the i-c-e-c-r-e-a-m I promised her earlier."

"Ice cream!" Cleo shouted, banging her heels on the sand.

Assata and I shared another smile.

"That's my cue," she said.

"Hope to see you around," I said. The ice was starting to do its numbing magic. "And thanks for the ice."

"Hope you feel better! Come on, Cleo."

Mom picked up the cooler, Cleo waved, and off they went, right as Stefon walked up again.

"Well?"

"No luck finding any of the big guys close enough to make a difference, but Rolf said he can be here in five minutes."

"Rolf? He's skinnier than Carlson!"

"Yeah, but he's strong," Stefon said, echoing the surfer's words. "And a lot less flaky."

I adjusted the ice pack and groaned again.

"Just tell him to meet us at the top of the cliff. If I can sit here with the ice for a few minutes, and you can clear the stairs ahead of me, I think I can make it."

"You sure, babe? I mean, I can carry you if it comes to that."

"Up all those stairs? No way. I can make it."

Which was probably a lie, but hey, a witch has to keep her dignity, and no way was my boyfriend—big and strong and knightly as he is—carrying my ample butt up all those stairs.

Three pug dogs raced in circles around us, panting joyfully.

"What is up with the dogs today?" Stefon said.

That made me smile.

"Everyone's getting ready for the Wag a Lot Fun Run! Oh no..."

"What," Stefon asked. "Did you injure something else?"

The pugs raced off, barking at the waves.

"I won't be able to do the run."

"Oh, babe, that's okay. You can still volunteer, can't you?"

"I guess," I sighed. Little did I know that being kept out of the 10K by a random dude and his dog was one of the best things that could have happened to me.

3

I was ensconced in a comfy leather club chair, feet propped on an ottoman, ice on my injured ankle. I was at the Blueberry Café, ignoring the warbling pop singer currently on rotation, and reading the latest Devon Monk urban fantasy.

My stomach growled at the mingled scents of cinnamon, bread, and coffee. One bad thing about a twisted ankle? I had to wait for Angie to deliver my usual tea and muffin. At least I was in a good spot.

Stefon, being the good boyfriend that he is, had taken good care of me the evening before. He fixed dinner, served me chocolate cherry ice cream, and reminded me to take a break from my ice pack every twenty minutes. My ankle wasn't as bad as I had feared, though I was limping, and yeah, no run. I had Stefon's old crutches and would definitely be needing them for a few days at the very least. Right now, they lay on the floor next to my chair, tucked out of the way of café traffic.

Speaking of traffic, I couldn't drive yet, which was a major pain, so Stefon dropped me off here at Angie's and then went back to his place. He was on yet another contract deadline and couldn't loll about drinking coffee. Stefon was a popular programmer who made a lot more money than me and spent it on high-tech gadgets, medieval stuff—including a large canvas tent, swords, and armor—and gaming gear of both the video and tabletop varieties.

Stefon also had a game to run that night, though he said if I needed him he would cancel. I had kissed him and told him to go be the Dungeon Master of everybody's dreams. If the quest didn't go too late, he would stop by my place.

I would be crutching up the street to work myself soon enough, but for now, was enjoying the "library" section of the Blueberry Café. It was tucked toward the back of the space, and had three comfy chairs with side tables, a couple of small, regular tables, and two sets of bookcases filled with offerings from local writers that folks could peruse as they drank coffee.

On the shelves were also discreet signs that read "Like what you're reading? Head to The Widening Gyre for more!"

That's how shops work in small towns: we all send customers to each other. The cash point at the bookshop has a cute "Book and Muffin Pairing of the Week" setup, with a ten-percent-off coupon for both the muffin and featured book. That was another brainstorm of Tabitha and Tracy. As I said, those teens earn their wages.

So far, I had the back end to myself, the other customers choosing to sit in the brighter main area, where sunlight streamed through large windows, lighting up the blond tables and matching chairs. I spied Delta Crabbit in her usual spot next to a window. The gray-haired witch surreptitiously slipped pieces of chocolate muffin into the tote bag on the chair next to her.

That was for Preston. He's a gnome. And while Seashell Cove locals might have their suspicions about gnomes and witches and the rest, we try to keep things on the down low for the tourists.

Partially because we don't want to freak them out, but the other reason? We don't want to be overrun by either flaky magic seekers or fire-toting zealots, ready to burn us out of house and home.

The ghosts are a different matter. The Historic Kelpie Inn has been cashing in on that for decades.

I flipped a page, willing my stomach to stop distracting me from what was a very fun paranormal book about a couple traveling Route 66.

Angie approached carrying a tray filled with my tea and what looked suspiciously like not-a-muffin. Angie is a little older than me, and about my size. She wore her usual uniform of a blue Blueberry Café apron tied over jeans and T-shirt. A blueberry-blue kerchief tied back her blond hair. She had a pleasant smile on her round-cheeked face.

"Having a good morning?" I asked.

"Yeah. We had a nice rush, no drama, and are well on our way with lunch prep. I tell you, having a new person in the kitchen is a big help. Clarita and I were being run ragged. Buster is a dream."

"Glad to hear it."

She plopped down a breakfast sandwich on the little table next to my chair, plus a strong cup of English Breakfast tea and a small jug of oat milk.

"Hey," I complained, "what about my muffin?"

"You're injured. You need protein, not just sugar."

I literally growled. If I'd been Rhiannon, she'd have gotten a swipe and hiss. I really like Angie's muffins.

Angie was nonplussed.

"If you're a good girl and eat your breakfast sandwich. I'll give you a muffin to go."

"Mo-om!" I rolled my eyes, complaining.

She just grinned and waltzed away. As soon as she was gone, I slid a Biff the Ghost bookmark into my book and set it aside.

Then I bit into the cheesy eggy goodness and blessed my friend for her foresight. She was right. This was just what I needed. And it was so. Freaking. Good.

Halfway through the uh-maze-ing sandwich, I heard a commotion at the door. It was Tabitha and Tracy, my two witchy assistants, and they practically bounced with excitement.

Tabitha was a Chinese American Wiccan with black hair cut in a sharp bob. Today, she was dressed in her usual Goth black jeans paired with pink high-top sneakers and a black T-shirt with a pink pentagram on it. Lately, she'd also gotten heavily into eyeliner.

Her bestie Tracy was as white as me, and the daughter of my witch colleague, Carol. Tracy has been training with me and Uncle Cyrus in the magical arts. Her long blond hair was loose around her shoulders, and she wore turquoise high tops, blue jeans, and a white Widening Gyre T-shirt with the ghost and a stack of books print. It matched the one I wore myself.

They looked around, then raced over to me, dodging around tables and the sugar and creamer station, heading straight toward the library.

"Sarah, are you okay?" Tabitha asked.

I shrugged.

"Um, well enough," I said, glancing down at the half sandwich still gripped in my hand. "If you two want something to eat or drink, you can tell Angie to put it on my tab."

"Cool!" Tracy said. They raced off to the counter.

I took another bite of sandwich just as Delta Crabbit shouted out "Watch out! No!"

I dropped my sandwich and looked toward Delta's table. She was standing, face pressed to the window, then shoved back her chair, grabbed her bulging tote bag, and barreled from the café into the street.

I leaned over to grab my crutches—dang my ankle!—as the teens looked back at me. I shooed them both toward the door. By the time I crutched my way through the café, they would have more intel for me than a double agent.

Giving my final two bites of sandwich and mug of cooling tea a longing glance, I shoved the crutches under my arms and lurched through the tables and curious onlookers, heading toward the café door.

4

By the time I got outside, Delta was careening through traffic and the teens were shouting. I could hear their voices, but the sidewalks were seriously jammed....

There they were, racing out between a van and one of those big shiny-clean work trucks that never seem to see a day of work.

"What is going on?" Angie joined me on the sidewalk.

"I have no idea!"

"Are those girls out of their minds?" a smooth voice interjected.

My head and Angie's both whipped around. There, looking dapper as always, was Uncle Cyrus. He's not really my uncle but had been a close friend of my parents and is more like family than anything else.

Including that "really annoying but I still love them to bits" thing that a lot of people get with their family members.

Today his dark skin was set off by blue linen trousers, a gleaming white linen shirt, and some sort of fancy

Italian leather sandals. A wristwatch that cost more than my yearly mortgage gleamed from his right wrist, picking up on the silver of his rings. To top it all off, a straw fedora perched on his smooth shaved head.

Cyrus was always way too fancy for our tiny burg.

"Did you just pop in?" I asked.

He just grinned inscrutably, not bothering to answer. Of course, he did. Dang warlocks and their ability to move through space as if they had a Star Trek transporter. Yeah. I was definitely jealous. Witches just don't have that skill in our magical arsenal.

"What are Tracy and Tabitha doing?" he asked, whipping on a pair of sunglasses.

"That's what we're trying to figure out," Angie said. "I'll go ask Delta."

She hurried toward the older witch. I spied a purple pointy hat and pale, round, bearded face peeking out from Delta's tote. Preston the gnome wanted in on the action, clearly. I just hope none of the tourists saw him and freaked out. Though I found that people usually thought he was a ceramic garden gnome, despite his tendency to scowl and stomp his feet at the slightest provocation.

What can I say? Most of the time, people see what they expect to see.

Tracy was crouched down, dealing with something, as Tabitha's dark bob whipped this way and that, clearly looking for something.

"Shall I?" asked Cyrus, gesturing across the street.

I looked down at my crutches and cursed that dang Frisbee. There was no way I was navigating through summer traffic on these crutches.

"Yes please."

Cyrus swanned through the cars as if he was sauntering down a French avenue. Not one person honked. As a matter of fact, I swore it looked as if a pathway appeared in front of him. And it probably did.

Darn him.

I eased up on my crutches. My arms were already getting sore, which did not bode well for crutching my way to the bookshop when whatever this was had finished.

Finally, Delta Crabbit and Angie approached, along with a burly white man with curly red hair, wearing a Blueberry Café apron.

"Hi, I'm Buster," he said, holding out his meaty hand for a shake.

Balanced on my crutches, I held out my own hand. When our skin touched, I felt a minor tingle and looked up at him, surprised.

Was that a look of satisfaction I saw flash by, quickly replaced by a friendly, innocent look? Was there yet another new magic worker in town who hadn't bothered to check in with the rest of us?

I held his light brown eyes for a moment, weighing my options, before deciding that now was not the time. I'd deal with Buster later. And talk with my uncle about the recent influx of unregistered magical types in Seashell Cove. There seemed to be more and more lately.

Across the busy street, Cyrus reached the teens.

"What happened?" I asked Delta. The witch at my side wrung her hands, looking worried and upset.

"A dog ran into traffic! It looked confused and lost."

Uh oh. "What kind of dog?"

"One of those silly yellow retrievers," Preston chimed in from his comfy perch inside the tote bag. Rhiannon had convinced Delta that the gnome needed a pillow in there. He was much more amenable to being carried around these days, and got along with Rhiannon better, too.

Turns out he used to thrash so much because he hated being jostled. Can't say that I blame him.

"That's bad," I said. "Where is Carlson?"

"Who's Carlson?" several voices said in concert.

I gestured at my ankle. "The surfer dude who threw the Frisbee at my head, causing this."

"No kidding?" Angie said. "What's this guy look like?"

"Tallish. Skinny. Blond. Board shorts. Surfer dude type. Looks like he belongs on a beach in Southern California. Not here."

Buster *humphed* behind me. Seemed as if Carlson had made an impression on more people than me.

I looked across the street. Uncle Cyrus held up one regal hand to stop traffic and Tabitha made way for Tracy, who walked half hunched, one hand clutching at Board Wax's collar. The dog looked happier than a kid with ice cream at all the attention.

And he had a Frisbee in his mouth.

"Board Wax!" I said.

"Board Wax?" Uncle Cyrus asked, stepping back onto the sidewalk.

The dog rushed toward me, heading directly for my crotch with that orange disc.

"Gah!" I swayed dangerously on my crutches. Luckily, Angie was there to steady me.

"No! Down!" Tabitha struggled to control the excitable pooch. Tracy bent to help, containing him by throwing two arms around his chest.

"Sit!" she said in her most commanding witch voice.

And dang if the dog didn't sit right down, as if it was what he wanted most in the world.

As if it was all his idea.

"Did you just...?" Had she really gotten into the dog's head and manipulated him that way? That was so out of bounds.

Tracy looked at me, an innocent look plastered on her face.

Cyrus *tsked*. "We'll talk about ethics at your lessons later. But for now? Good job."

I glared at my uncle. He was giving Tracy bad ideas, rewarding her for behavior like this.

He just stared back from behind those sunglasses. "As if you didn't do worse when you were her age."

Like I said. Annoying.

I sputtered, searching for a reply, when Delta raised a hand.

"Stop this. We have no time for your petty disagreements."

Delta turned to me. "You clearly know this animal. Why is it running loose in the streets?"

"He could have gotten hurt!" Tracy said. "Couldn't you, boy?"

Board Wax just panted happily and gnawed on the orange Frisbee.

"He belongs to a guy named Carlson who almost brained me with that Frisbee yesterday. Where he's gotten to, I don't know."

Tracy stood, and whipped out her phone, texting madly.

"Who are you texting?" Tabitha asked, still crouched next to the happy dog.

"My mom. Gonna see if she'll let us take him. At least

until we find his rightful human."

The teens cracked me up. Rightful human. Like, that was how they talked.

But they were also good-hearted, and I loved them for it.

"We'll need to leave a notice somewhere, telling Carlson we have his dog," I said.

"I don't suppose..." Delta looked hopeful.

"That I got his phone number? No. I was in a lot of pain at the time. All I wanted was for him to get away from me."

But I was regretting it now.

"Do you think he's in town for the Wag a Lot?" Tabitha asked.

"Wag. A. Lot." Uncle Cyrus repeated, as if he understood that those three sounds were words but had no idea why they were strung together.

"It's a charity for our local shelter," I replied. "A fun run. It's a big deal that happens every year. I'm surprised you don't remember."

"Anything that has to do with running is a thing I try my best to forget," he said, cheating the dark glasses down his nose and peering at me. "Were you going to join in this..." he waved a hand "...festive event?"

I sighed. My ankle was really starting to throb from the lack of being propped on a soft cushion.

"I was, until Board Wax and Carlson came along."

So now, not only was I not able to do the 10K, I had a stray dog and possibly missing owner—or rightful human—to contend with.

And in a town crammed with tourists, how were we going to track down one skinny blond surfer with a distinct lack of adulting skills?

5

::Y::*ou are not keeping that dog.::*
Cyrus had popped off to who knows where, and the rest of us were back in the bookshop. Rhiannon was not pleased. We had interrupted her mid-nap, causing her to go full on Halloween cat when she saw the rambunctious retriever, tongue lolling and tail wagging. Now that the teens had taken Board Wax back to the kitchenette to get him some water and make tea, her fur was smooth again, but barely.

"We can't just let him race around town unattended during tourist season," I replied.

"Excuse me?" a startled woman said, almost dropping the latest Gabino Iglesias novel.

"Just talking to myself. I do that sometimes. Can I help you find anything else?"

Rhiannon sneezed, then set about washing herself for the umpteenth time, leaving black hairs on the window display. If she didn't bring in customers...

Oh, who am I kidding. I love that dang cat, and that's what handheld vacuum devices are for, right?

"I think I'm good," the woman replied. "Just finished the one book I brought on our trip and needed a fix."

"Well, you picked a good one! I don't read horror, but I've heard nothing but good things about his writing." I crutched to the cash point, rang her up, and sent her on her way.

Duncan swanned in, bleached-blond head down, checking something on his phone. Today's T-shirt was an old *Where the Wild Things Are* classic, with monsters swinging from trees.

"Hey boss," he said, looking up. Then his eyes widened behind his heavy, black-framed retro glasses. "What happened to you? It was jogging, wasn't it? I always say that stuff will kill you."

I laughed. "Not everyone is cut out to be a total couch potato, Duncan. And it was a Frisbee accident."

Just then, Board Wax barked in the kitchenette.

Duncan's head snapped toward the back.

"Sarah? Is there a d-o-g here?"

He glanced uneasily at Rhiannon, now glaring from the front window display. She hopped down and bumped his jeans-clad shins. He bent to pay proper tribute.

"There is a d-o-g, and the c-a-t already saw him, so, no need to spell."

::*There is a dog. And it is a terrible, large, slobbering beast!*:: she yowled.

"Huh. Guess Rhiannon isn't too happy about it, are you girl? Wonder what you'd be saying if you spoke English."

I just smiled, noncommittally. "If you're good here, I'm going to go check on the teens."

"Sure thing." He was already fiddling with the computer, looking at online orders

I headed back to the kitchenette, with my step thump, step thump gait announcing my arrival to all and sundry, armpits complaining. I hadn't even been on crutches for a full day and I was already whining.

I really needed to get over myself, didn't I?

::*You do.*:: Rhiannon mind-thought.

::*Hey, stay out of my head!*:: I shouted back.

::*Hmph,*:: she replied, but then fell thankfully silent.

Well, that was new. Could Rhiannon really read my mind all the time? I clearly needed to tighten up my psychic wards and protections.

Propping myself on one crutch, I leaned forward to open the kitchenette door, pretty proud of myself at not overbalancing.

As soon as the door opened, though, I realized my mistake.

Board Wax's cheerful yellow head slammed directly into my crotch, almost toppling me backwards. I braced myself against the door jamb, swaying dangerously as the dog continued his joyous assault.

"Board Wax! No!" Tracy shouted, and grabbed his collar.

Tabitha turned from where she was making tea.

"Hey boss, you okay?"

"I'm fine." I sighed. "But I have no idea what we're going to do about this dog."

Board Wax wagged his fluffy golden tail and slurped noisily at a plastic bowl of water the teens had sat down for him.

"I asked my mom if we could take him for a few days," Tracy said.

"And?"

"She said it would be okay if I agreed to take care of him, you know, walk him, and feed him, and stuff."

"And pick up his poop," Tabitha said with a cackle, dark bob swaying around her slender shoulders.

Tracy just rolled her eyes.

"Is the tea almost ready?" I asked. I hadn't finished my cup at Angie's.

"Sure is," Tabitha replied, getting everything onto the tea tray.

"All right. Let's go talk about this before the store gets too busy."

Though in summer, that could be five minutes from now. But I'd take whatever time sitting down I could. I crutched my way over to the comfortable striped chairs set beneath a stained glass window showing a stack of books with brightly colored spines.

A low table sat between the chairs, used by customers for the stacks of books they were perusing as they tried to figure out what to buy.

I know some bookstores think letting people sit and read is bad for business, but I've found the opposite is true. If people read for ten minutes, getting hooked on an interesting slice of history, or the latest summer read, they're more likely to buy. My dad taught me that.

Tracy and Tabitha came back out, thankfully leaving Board Wax shut in the kitchenette.

Tabitha set the tea tray down on the table and Tracy grabbed another chair.

"So," Tracy said, tying her long blond hair back in a ponytail. "I can take Board Wax home, but that still doesn't help us figure out what to do with him long term."

"Or how to figure out what happened to his human," Tabitha said.

I rubbed the bridge of my nose where it met my fore-head and the dull ache starting there.

"That's the problem, isn't it?" I said. "I mean, all we have is the guy's first name and his dog... Oh wait. Did you check the collar? Does Board Wax have a tag with a phone number on it?

"Brilliant!"

Tracy raced back to the kitchen as Tabitha leaned forward to pour the tea, adding a splash of oat milk to mine, and half a spoonful of sugar to her own.

I settled back with the warm cup in hand, grateful for my life. Then my ankle throbbed, reminding me that I needed to prop it up again.

"Tabitha, can you get me...?" I gestured toward my lower leg.

"Oh, sure, boss. Coming right up."

This was a new thing, all of them calling me boss. I knew it was affectionate, but I wasn't sure I liked it. It reminded me too much of the fact that my dad was no longer with me. Mom either, though she had died enough years ago that I was used to it. But dad stuff? That still really hit me sometimes.

"There was a phone number," Tracy said, coming back just as Tabitha returned with a one of the low chairs from the children's section and an extra pillow. I got my ankle propped, and everyone sat down.

Tracy punched numbers into her phone and held it to her ear. I drank my tea and waited.

Tabitha looked kind of distant. Far away. I wondered if everything was okay with her. We had only found out recently that her parents were vampires, and I wondered if that was causing her trouble.

"Nothing," Tracy said. "They're not picking up."

"Just text them," said Tabitha. "Tell them we have their dog."

Tracy rolled her eyes at her friend.

"Thanks, Captain Obvious."

"Just saying." Tabitha grinned and sipped her tea.

The front bells clattered. We all looked up. Waiting.

"Hi, Duncan." That was Delta Crabbit's voice.

"Tracy, could you...?'

"On it." She scurried off to find another chair. With as often as we used this nook as a meeting spot, I might need to rethink the furniture situation.

Delta looked harried, gray hair sticking out all over as if she'd combed it with an egg beater. The tip of Preston's purple cap poked up from the tote bag.

Tracy was back with the chair.

"I'll get another cup," she said.

"Two cups, please!" Preston called out.

Delta sat with a huff and carefully set the tote down on the ground. The gnome popped out and adjusted his purple cap with his fat little fingers.

"Finally," he said. "I feel as if I've been in that bag all day. You keep dragging me hither and yon..."

"Oh, quiet, gnome. At least you get carried. I'm the one doing all the walking."

I smothered a grin with my tea mug. The longer they were friends, the more Delta and Preston seemed like an old married couple.

"Any news?" I asked.

Tracy carefully filled the human-sized and gnome-sized mugs and handed them out.

Delta raked a hand through her hair and blew on her tea before taking a hefty gulp and settling back in the chair. Story time.

"Preston and I went exploring. We walked up and down Main Street and then went to the beach where you said you took your fall, and..."

She set her mug down and leaned over to rummage through the tote bag, emerging with a battered orange cloth sneaker.

"We found this. Do you recognize it?"

I peered at the shoe, a well-worn canvas sneaker in a faded orange. It was the type my dad used to call tennies. I racked my memory.

"I think that was what Carlson was wearing. But I can't be sure. I was a little preoccupied with my ankle." And with how the heck I was going to get off that beach, an ordeal I would rather not relive, quite frankly

"How are you at psychometry?" Delta asked. "I was never much good at it."

"Psychometry?" Tabitha said. "That's excellent. We haven't learned about that yet."

Both girls took out their phones, ready to take notes.

I waved my hands.

"We are not doing the lesson in psychometry right now." I turned to Delta. "I'm okay at psychometry, but Cyrus is even better."

And where the heck had he gone, anyway? Drat that warlock.

"Ooh, ooh!" Tracy bounced in her chair, tea sloshing perilously. "Can we do it tonight at your house?"

I looked at her expectant face shining with excitement. I swear, I'm only in my late twenties, but sometimes teenagers make me feel old.

"I guess so," I said.

I mean, why not? Stefon was busy running his game, my ex-girlfriend turned best friend, Cecilia, was busy with

Toby, and my plans for the evening? They were watching *Charmed* reruns from the comfort of my couch while eating my weight in caramel ice cream.

Tracy looked at her phone, then at Tabitha.

"My mom's here to pick up Board Wax. You coming?"

"Wait, *neither* of you are working today?" I asked.

"Well, we can't exactly leave the dog locked in the kitchen...."

"I'll stay, Sarah," Tabitha said, then glanced back at her friend. "Can you maybe come pick me up for dinner?"

Tracy nodded. "Sure. I'll text you later. Can you help me get Board Wax?"

The teens loped off through the bookcases, and Delta frowned.

"I hope this abandoned shoe doesn't portend something bad."

I did, too.

But it felt doubtful.

6

Tabitha, Tracy, and Tracy's mother, Carol,—another blond—crowded on the sofa in the cozy cottage I call home. It started out as my parents' place, becoming Dad's after my mom's death. And then...when Dad's own health was failing, it became mine. Someday I would get around to redecorating, but for now, the old, well-worn furniture did the trick.

Uncle Cyrus and I sat in the chairs opposite the couch, fireplace behind us and the coffee table in the center. My feet were propped on a leather ottoman, and I'd changed into comfy sweatpants and had a glass of soda water close to hand.

Cyrus, dressed in his somehow-still-crisp linen sat, legs crossed, hands relaxed on the arms of the chair. He stared at the battered coffee table with distaste. Well, not at the coffee table, exactly, but at the battered orange sneaker sitting smack dab in the center of it. At least the teens had put down a washable placemat underneath it. Who knows where the shoe had been?

"So," Tracy said, ever eager to learn. "You're going to teach us psychometry?"

Uncle Cyrus tapped his long, elegant fingers on the chair arms and then dragged his gaze away from the offending shoe, coming to rest on Tracy's bright, open face.

"Psychometry. Yes. Psychometry, simply put, is gathering psychic information from an object."

"So how does it work?" Tabitha asked, leaning forward. Tabitha always wanted to get down to the basics of how things worked. A Wiccan by religion, the young Goth should have just been along for the ride. But if you ask me, she was a better student than hereditary witch Tracy.

It made me wonder if a regular human could grow into some of our powers. Oh, I mean, I know plenty of Wiccans who pack quite a psychic punch, and psychometry was certainly something Tabitha could learn.... But elemental magic the way witches did it? I didn't think so.

Uncle Cyrus snapped his fingers in front of my face.

"What?" I asked.

"You were wandering," he said. "Are you certain you're up for this?"

"I'm fine," I groused, then adjusted my foot on the ottoman. My ankle still hurt like heck but I didn't need to let Cyrus know that.

"So how does it work?" Tracy asked.

"Like any other psychic skill," Cyrus said. "Just the way your mother taught you."

And the way Cyrus and I had been helping Tracy refine.

"You center yourself," he continued. "Slow down your breathing and then slowly open up your psychic centers to whatever it is you are touching or holding in your hands."

"So, you can teach us, right?" Tracy asked.

"We shall see."

"Oh, come on, Cyrus, loosen up," I said. "Yes, we can teach you."

Now it was Carol's turn to lean toward the two teens.

"Some people are more naturally inclined toward that skill, but that doesn't mean that with practice, you can't develop it."

"Carol is right. All the psychic skills are teachable." I turned back to my uncle. "Cyrus, I think the best thing to do is just show them first. We can go over the fundamentals later."

In other words, get the show on the road, warlock. He gave me a small frown, which told me he picked up on my energy if not my words. I ignored the look and took a drink of my bubbly water.

Just as Cyrus reached forward for the shoe, a barking started up from my backyard, where Board Wax was on a grassy patch, tethered to my small back porch.

"That dog." Carol sighed. "I didn't know what I was getting myself into."

"I'll check on him!" Tracy said, bouncing up. "Don't start without me!"

"I'm sorry you have to deal with that animal again," Carol said to me. "I mean, he's good-tempered, but a bit of a lummox. Is your ankle going to be all right?"

I shrugged. "It should be. But I'm going to miss the Wag a Lot run."

Uncle Cyrus practically shuddered, but blessedly didn't comment this time, which was good, because his opinions on running were annoying, and because there was a sudden clatter of toenails on the kitchen floor.

Board Wax's grinning face appeared, followed by that golden frond of a tail, swinging wildly toward my father's mementos. Tracy was doing her best to get him to heel, but it looked like a lost cause.

Luckily, she steered the lummox away from my chair before I got a wet nose in my crotch again.

"Now you have to be good," Tracy said. "Sit."

Board Wax sat next to the end of the couch and thunked his big head on the arm, begging for pets. Tracy obliged.

"Are we quite through?" Cyrus asked.

I dragged my attention back to the task at hand, and spoke.

"Let's all center." I certainly needed to. "Feet flat on the floor unless you're me. Palms up and open. Spine floating from your pelvis... Now slow your breathing down. Drop into the stillness that is your center."

The energy in the room shifted as every witch, Wiccan, and warlock followed my instructions.

Starting a centering meditation is like ringing Pavlov's bell. You start the breathing countdown or say the words "find your center" and every witch within a mile snaps to.

"Feel the energy bodies that rest around your physical form, and send a breath outward, filling your aura. Ask any guides you have to be present." The room grew a little more crowded as people's ancestor helpers or spirit guides showed up. I could feel the strange energies tingling along my skin.

"Soften your gaze...and open to the orange sneaker."

Uncle Cyrus picked it up, gently cradling the shoe in both of his hands.

His breathing deepened, and I swore I could feel his energy fields vibrate as he tuned in to the ugly shoe.

"Sand," he said. "Salt water."

Then his mouth turned down. "Dog."

Board Wax thumped his tail, and Cyrus went quiet.

"Anything else?" Carol prompted. The blond-haired witch had her eyes fixed on the orange shoe. I could tell she was tuning in to something despite not having her hands on the object. Carol had more than a touch of clairvoyance, meaning, she Saw things. I was more clairaudient, which meant I Heard more things than I ever wanted to.

"Are you picking up on something?" I asked her.

"Unhappiness," she said. "An unhappy man pretending to be otherwise. A man involved in secrets. Surrounded by secrets, and spouting lies."

Carol fell silent. The teens' eyes were wide open, soaking it all in.

Cyrus took a shuddering breath, and I could feel him open to the shoe on a deeper level.

"I see hands exchanging money," he said. "Money and something..."

His fingertips rubbed together as if trying to feel what he was seeing.

"Something small. Something encased in plastic film."

"Like drugs?" Tracy asked.

Carol's eyes shot open and looked at her daughter.

"What?" Tracy said. "I watch movies."

Tabitha smirked, but wisely kept her mouth shut.

But drugs? That was an interesting development.

Cyrus licked his lips and nodded.

"I believe so. Or something like drugs. And some people around the man are very angry. I hear buzzing sounds..." He fell silent again, and we all waited in the hush of my living room.

Buzzing. What buzzed? Tattoo parlors buzzed. Bees... what else? But I didn't want to break Cyrus's concentration by asking.

The only sounds were Board Wax's panting and the thump of his tail.

Finally, Cyrus's eyes opened and he blinked, shoulders relaxing. He carefully set the shoe down on the table.

"Did you get anything else?" I asked.

"I'm not certain. There was a swirl of activity, energy, and emotion. The only thing I know for sure is this: person who last wore this shoe is either in grave danger or already dead."

7

Stomach growling, I sat across the table at the Vargas's Tamale Parlor with my ex-girlfriend, now best friend, Cecilia. The table had a glass top that covered a turquoise blue serape, and most importantly, had a large bowl filled with freshly made tortilla chips and two bowls of salsa in the middle.

Despite being slammed, it had been a thankfully uneventful day at the bookshop. I'd managed to spend most of my time propped up behind the counter, while Duncan and the teens ran around helping people, and replacing stock...and encouraging visitors to take photos in front of the ghostly mirror to post on social media. The teens were relentless, but as I've said, I can't complain.

Among the customers were Assata—the woman from the beach— and her cute toddler, Chloe, who was very excited about the promised book. I had asked Assata if she'd seen Carlson around town anywhere, but she'd just frowned, shaking her head. So much for my sleuthing.

The day rushed by with more customers and the constant chatter of people buying books or asking for directions around our pocket-sized town. The town's tarot reader, Jerry Hamamoto, came in with his son, Ash, to pick up another dragon book. I only had a few minutes to chat before they, too, went on their way.

If I hadn't been sitting down all day, I would say that I'd been run off my feet. As it was, I hadn't taken a lunch break and was more than ready for dinner.

Cecilia munched a chip loaded with green tomatillo salsa in her small mouth. For as tiny as she is, the woman can eat. But then, she does physical labor for a living. Cecilia, with her fuchsia hair, black kohl-lined eyes, and smooth skin is a pretty fabulous person. And I'm not just saying that because she's my ex.

She's Asian-American, and a bad-ass auto mechanic with fabulous fashion sense. Today's outfit of burgundy boots, black skinny jeans, and a complicated white cotton wrap shirt is just one example. When not wearing coveralls, Cecilia dresses as some combination of punk, Goth, and fashion maven Esther Quek crossed with a Japanese club kid.

She is my favorite person besides Stefon.

Glasses of horchata sweated on the table in front of us as we perused the large, plastic-coated menus, though why we bothered, I wasn't sure. After all these years, we had the thing memorized.

David, the owner's son, came by, dark hair neatly combed, red apron over his black slacks and white shirt.

"Ready to order?" he asked.

"Chili rellenos for me," Cecilia said.

"I'd like the tamale special, please."

"Coming right up." He walked away, pausing to talk with two diners at another table who were excitedly gesturing at something. They all laughed, and David headed back to the kitchen, where Mrs. Vargas was sure to be cooking up a storm.

"Toby couldn't make it?" I asked.

A frown creased her otherwise unmarred skin, creating a slight vee between her perfect eyebrows.

"No. They decided to stay home because the garden sprites are freaking out again."

Uh oh. The last time the sprites had acted up, it was because of murder.

We both took a sip of the milky, cinnamon rice drink. She was clearly thinking, and I knew that sometimes I had to wait things out to get the story.

"Toby wanted me to talk to you about it, as a matter of fact."

Cecilia's partner, Toby, was a hob, which is kind of a domestic fae. They kept the cottage kitchen spotless, baked terrific bread and scones, and had a knack for the kitchen garden as well. The sprites loved hanging out in Toby's garden, and I couldn't blame them.

Toby was nonbinary, which had raised a few eyebrows in town at first, but people got over it, which was a good thing. This also paved the way for young Ash, Jerry's son, who was trans. Our little seaside village was getting used to the twenty-first century, where people had more freedom to be who they truly were. Luckily, Seashell Cove had long had a live-and-let-live attitude, probably because so many artists lived here. And because we have centaurs in the forest just outside town. And gnomes. And sprites. And witches. And...you get the idea.

I'd have to ask some of the old ghosts at the Kelpie which had come first, though. The artists or the magical creatures. The two seemed to feed one another, creating a happy symbiosis.

Some of the neighboring towns were less open-minded. Let's just say that I loved Seashell Cove and was staying here.

"Why did they want to talk to me? And what's wrong with the sprites? Are they okay?"

Now it was my turn to frown.

"None of them died, did they?"

Cecilia waved a hand. "No. Nothing like that, thank my Chinese ancestors. But the head sprite Rowena wants a meeting with you. I'm kind of acting as emissary."

She sipped her horchata and looked out the window the ocean.

"Cecilia, you have to tell me what's going on."

"I know. I know," she said. She toyed with a chip, staring at it as if it were a foreign object before popping it into her mouth. While I waited for her to finish crunching, I loaded some salsa fresca on a chip of my own.

Heaven.

"It's just that I don't exactly know how to explain it..."

I swallowed my mouthful of goodness.

"So don't explain it. Just spit it out."

"Apparently Rowena and the others are upset because someone is stealing faery dust."

"Faery dust? That's real?" I mean, I recalled from my lessons that sprites had a powdery coating on their wings like butterflies did, but never thought it had any utility beyond that.

Cecilia puffed out in annoyance. "Of course, it's real. Do you pay attention to anything going on this town? I thought you're supposed to be Justice."

I waved my hands in the air between us. "Whoa, my friend. I get that you're upset, but that's no reason to be snippy with me."

Besides, I'd never asked to be Justice in the first place. As soon as I passed my ordeal of a test, making me a full-fledged witch, I learned that it came with a new job. Not for every witch, oh no, but just for me. The job of Justice was one that each of my parents had held in the past. It was part magical investigator and often judge and jury as well.

It wasn't a job I relished, but luckily, I had a good team around me. Cecilia included. So, I didn't have to do it alone.

No one should mete out justice on their own.

It takes a village, right?

Cecilia grumbled and stuffed a loaded chip into her tiny mouth.

"I've been a little distracted with the summer rush and all, and now my ankle."

Cecilia paused mid bite to nod in sympathy, then patted my hand.

"I get it. I'm sorry I was so harsh. It's just, Toby's so worried, and that makes me worry too."

"So, faery dust."

"Yeah," Cecilia said, "the way Toby explained it, is that it's some combination of magic and something else that they couldn't really explain, but it gives the fae their longevity and, you know, shine."

A rush of memory filled me, and I smacked a hand against my forehead.

"Ouch." Too hard. "I'm such a dope. I remember now. It was in my magic books somewhere but I'd forgotten. And they do kind of sparkle."

"Yeah." She nodded her head enthusiastically, fuchsia-colored hair bobbing around her face. "Apparently, that's something to do with the magic in the faery dust."

I chewed another chip.

"And you say that dust is missing?"

She nodded again, sipping her sweetened rice drink. "So, can you come over? Meet with Toby and the sprites?"

Just then, Davíd came back with our food. The heaping plates smelled mouthwatering, as usual. But seeing Davíd gave me an idea.

"Hey, Davíd?" I asked before he could walk away.

"Yeah, what's up?"

I lowered my voice. The restaurant wasn't crowded, because it was still a little early, but people were seated at a few tables nearby.

"Do the chaneques seem okay lately?"

He looked out the windows that faced the courtyard, and the chaneques' rock garden.

"Actually, I haven't seen them around much lately. I just figured they were hiding from the tourists."

"Do you mind if we talk to them? Can you act as interpreter?"

The stocky little fae spirits only spoke some form of sign, which I had so far failed to pick up.

"Of course. I'm due for a break soon anyway. Let me know when you're done eating."

"That'd be great," I said. Davíd loped back to the kitchen as Cecilia and I tucked into our food.

Mine oozed with cheesy goodness and just the right amount of spice.

Mrs. Vargas was one heck of a cook. The whole Vargas family might as well be magical as far as I was concerned. They all had amazing skills and talents. Davíd was super good with people, which is why he worked front of the house. His mom was an expert cook, and his dad? Let's just say Mr. Vargas had a way with plants and ran the most successful gardening business this part of the coast.

"How are things going at the shop?" I asked.

"Good. The classic cars are back in town again and Raul is in his element. We've seen some real beauties in... At least one or two of them always break down during the season."

Like I said, Cecilia was a mechanic who worked for Raul, the former shop teacher at our high school before leaving to open his own classic car garage. He not only hired my pansexual ex but it turns out he's gay himself. Like I said, for such a tiny town, we're pretty diverse.

"I have to admit," I said, swiping at my face with a heavy paper napkin, "all I wanted was a night off from weirdness to eat a good dinner with my best friend. But I'm getting pretty antsy to figure this thing out."

I took a final bite as Cecilia grinned at me from beneath her fuchsia-colored bangs, dark eyes crinkling at the corners.

"I knew you would say that, and here comes Davíd. Looks like he's ready for his break."

We paid up, and then I laboriously crutched my way out the door to the outside patio where Mr. Vargas had helped the fae land spirits known as the chaneques to build a beautiful rock garden, interspersed with native plants that were hardy enough to withstand the scraping winds that came in off the ocean.

I saw some movement near what I thought of as the grotto at the back of the garden. The rock formation was the entryway to the underground warren the chaneques called home.

"All right," I said, "let's do this."

8

Cecilia crouched next to the rock cairn, braced on her burgundy boots.

"Hello-o," she called out. "Anybody home?"

"Hola!" Davíd said, leaning toward the opening between two small boulders.

I heard scrabbling, a small clank, and then the crunching stomp of tiny boots as two chaneques way emerged from the gloom, blinking in the summer sun.

Chaneques are sort of fae garden spirits. Short, stocky, and square-headed, with dark brown skin and darker eyes. These two wore practical clothing in shades of earth-brown and green and stood between two and three feet tall.

The first one, which I recognized as the leader from my other dealings with these creatures, signed something.

I looked at Davíd for a translation.

He just stared at the chaneques, concentrating hard.

The lead one signed something back, clearly in conversation.

"What's happening?" I asked Davíd.

"I was telling them that something had upset you."

He turned back to the little gardeners and seemed to both speak out loud and with his mind at the same time.

"This one here, brings news from the sprites." He pointed at Cecilia. "Someone has stolen their faery dust."

Both chaneques looked at each other and stomped their boots in anger.

"Can you tell us what has been happening here?" Davíd asked.

He stood for a moment as both chaneques gestured.

"He says that someone has been rearranging their rocks and lurking about...." Davíd tilted his head before continuing. "They think the person was searching for something."

"Can you describe them?" I asked, leaning against my crutches and looking at the lead chaneque.

"There was a big dog," Davíd translated. "Gold like the sun. And a man with pale skin and orange shoes."

Davíd turned to me.

"Does that mean anything to you?"

"Yes. That's Carlson, our missing surfer dude and his dog, Board Wax."

And the case just got weirder.

On the sidewalk just past the courtyard, three dogs ran past—an assortment of mutts—yipping wildly, leashes trailing behind their scampering legs. A white woman in a floppy hat and jeans raced after them, huffing and puffing.

"Got them!" Cecilia shouted, and sprang into action, fuchsia hair flying, chasing after the trio. She was fast, reaching out and grabbing first one leash, then a second.

Once she tugged those two to a stop, the third dog realized its friends were no longer free and circled back, tongue lolling. Cecilia led them back to the little court-yard garden.

"Thank you so much!" said the woman. She was wearing a Seashell Cove Pet Shelter T-shirt. I'd seen her around town before.

"They bolted so suddenly! They never do that. Do you, girls? You're usually such good walkers."

"They be excited for the Wag a Lot Fun Run," I remarked. "I'm Sarah, by the way."

The woman's face cleared. "Oh yes. Are you going to that? And my name is Rachel."

I gestured toward my crutches. "I intended to run but…"

"Well, we still need volunteers, and if your ankle is better in time, you could always do the 1K Puppy Run."

"I'll think about it," I said, "though I have a cat, not a dog."

The woman laughed. "Well, I don't think that would work out too well. Even if your cat does go on leash…"

"Probably not."

I smiled just to think of Rhiannon agreeing to a leash. No way. Plus, being surrounded by all those dogs? She would probably claw my arms to shreds and then not speak to me for a month.

Although that last might not be too bad of an idea.

Maybe I'd ask her after all.

I looked back at the courtyard. The chaneques had ducked back into their cave as soon as the dogs raced by. I didn't blame them for not welcoming the canine disruption.

If a dog managed to find their cave entrance, that could spell disaster.

"I'd better get these three back," said Rachel. "Hope to see you all around."

We waved off woman and dogs and David began walking back toward the restaurant.

"Hey, David," I said, "thanks for the information. And tell your mother the food was delicious as always."

"I will," he said, then pushed back inside. "Hasta luego."

And then it was just me and my best friend, standing in the Vargas's courtyard as Seashell Cove went about its business up and down the street.

I was suddenly exhausted.

"Cecilia, can you drive me home? I really need to get off my foot."

And to think about all the components of this case. Nothing was making sense. Yet.

"Sure thing," she said.

Cecilia and I headed next door to the Widening Gyre's tiny parking lot, where she'd left her mint condition, fancy muscle car. I should be able to tell you what kind it is. All I know is it's beautiful and teal blue, with the world's shiniest chrome and a V-8 engine.

I only know that last part because I once asked why the car was so dang loud.

It was the Cecilia's pride and joy and she'd rebuilt the whole thing herself.

Getting into it was kind of a pain with the crutches, but I managed. Once we were settled in the leather seats, I sighed. So roomy and comfortable.

"I really need to get a bigger car," I said.

I loved my bright orange electric Fiat to bits, but it was really too small for my ample frame. And whenever

Stefon and I went on a date he always had to drive, because no way were both of us fitting in that car.

"I've been telling you that for years," Cecilia said, clicking the key and engaging the engine with a rumble. "I can hook you up, you know."

"I don't know if I'm ready for a classic car," I said. "I was thinking more along the lines of an SUV."

"Boooring," she said.

"Or a Prius." I grinned and looked sideways to see her shudder. I knew that one would hurt a gearhead like her.

"In that case, I'll be happy to key the paint job on your shiny new car."

"Snob!"

Cecilia laughed, cranked up some old school punk music, and off we went.

9

I t was the next day, and my ankle was no better, but I
had things to do.

At some point in the coming week, I needed to drop by
The Historic Kelpie to sign up as a Wag a Lot volunteer,
but first?

I needed to do some investigating. So, I was standing
in front of Ancient Treasures

Stefon had dropped me off with a kiss and then headed
back to his place to work. I peered at the big windows
displaying fossils, wooden Dino puzzles, and other curios.
The flag and fake dino skeleton weren't out front yet
because it was too early for opening. But finally, I saw
movement toward the back of the shop. Tetris was in. Good.

Ever since his girlfriend died, several of his friends in
Seashell Cove had taken it upon ourselves to check in
with Tetris from time to time. Make sure he was okay. Not
sinking into the doldrums.

I put my shoulder to the door, surprised to find it
unlocked, and was greeted by the roar of a T. Rex. Not that

anyone knows what a T. Rex sounds like, but it's a fun novelty and keeps the tourist kiddos entertained.

"Sarah!" Tetris greeted me from behind the back counter where he was arranging a fossil display. "Guess I forgot to relock the door when I came in."

I slowly made my way toward the back.

"I heard you hurt yourself," he said. "How are you?"

"Well enough," I said, "all things considered. Busy, which is good, but I hate being slowed down like this."

I gestured toward the offending ankle.

"That's a drag. Let me know if there's something I can do to help. Meanwhile, what brings you to my shop today?"

I crutched past the display of miniature dinosaur skeletons and some beautiful seashells as he walked towards me, meeting me halfway.

"Here," he said, dragging a stool out from behind his cash point. "Pull up a chair."

"Thank you, Tetris." I hoisted myself onto the padded stool with a sigh of relief. "I came because there seems to be a missing person in town, and I wondered if you might know anything."

"Missing person?" he said. Taking out a rag and some vinegar cleaner, he started polishing the tops of the glass display cases. That had to be a never-ending chore in a store like his.

"Why do you think I would know anything about it?"

I shrugged. "I'm not sure, actually. He just seemed like a guy that might get along with you. You know?"

Though I suddenly doubted myself. Tetris was no surfer dude. Instead, he was a middle-aged punk rocker. Today's uniform was an ancient Crass T-shirt, once-black jeans now faded to gray, and his regulation battered black Doc Martens boots.

"Although, you two aren't alike. Not exactly. This guy was more of a surfer type. Seemed mellow. Had a golden retriever?"

"Oh yeah! He came in, browsed around. I gave him a bowl of water for his dog. He leashed him outside. Wow, man...he's missing?"

"Looks that way," I said. "Delta Crabbit found one of his shoes on the beach. Or at least we think it's his. And he's the reason I got hurt."

"What?"

"Frisbee. Dog. Driftwood. My ankle."

He waved his hands, rag flapping. "Say no more. But ouch!"

He resumed cleaning, as if waiting for me to say something else, but I wasn't sure how to approach the rest of the conversation. I mean, Tetris might not be into magic himself, but he's been around Seashell Cove long enough and been my friend long enough to have experienced plenty of what some people call the *woo*.

And his former girlfriend is now a ghost, one of the many that haunts The Historic Kelpie Inn, but that's a story for another day.

"Just spit it out," he said. "I know there's something you're not telling me, and it's probably something to do with magic."

"You're too wise, my friend." I adjusted myself on the padded stool. "Uncle Cyrus did some psychometry on the shoe—a little psychic exploration—and he seems to think Carlson is in trouble."

Tetris paused to scratch the pale stubble on his chin.

"What kind of trouble?"

"Again, we don't know. But he also saw money passing hands and tiny plastic baggies."

Tetris smacked his palms down on the glass counter, obliterating all the polishing he had just done with fresh fingerprints.

"I *knew* there was something about that guy. He kept hinting at things...but you know how it is when you're busy. You're helping customers and just trying to be friendly to the weird guy."

"Oh, I know it." We all did. It was part and parcel of running a store in a seasonal tourist town.

"You think he was trying to sell you drugs?" I asked.

"I don't know. Something like that. He seemed strange. But I just chalked it up to him being a friendly gregarious dude, you know?"

Well, he was that. Even after almost bonking me with his danged Frisbee.

"Anyway, I can help if you want," he said. "I mean, with your ankle and all. And with finding this guy."

"Well..." I said, thinking. "Thanks for the offer, Tetris. For right now, Stefon seems happy to drop me places, but if he gets tired of it..."

"Anytime," Tetris said. "Happy to drive you."

I smiled, hoping he didn't see I was faking. While it was nice of him to offer, considering that Tetris drove a forty-year-old truck that rattled and wheezed, I would rather make do with other people's vehicles. Tetris's truck was more junker than classic, if you know what I mean.

"Mostly, just keep your eyes and ears open. Also, do you know anyone who wants a dog?"

He looked sorrowful. "The golden retriever?"

I nodded.

"Oh man, that was such a sweet dog. Who's got him now?"

"Tracy, but I don't think Carol's too happy about the situation."

"Well, if that dog needs a place to stay, you let me know. He can come here and stay with me as long as he likes."

My shoulders dropped with relief. I hadn't even known I was hunching them. Some tension in my belly uncoiled itself, too.

"Tetris, that would be great. I'll tell Tracy today. She'll be disappointed, but I bet Carol will be by to thank you."

"No problem. I'm an old dog myself."

We both chuckled.

"All right, I better be moving on if I'm going to get to Angie's before opening the store."

I boosted my butt off the stool and grabbed my crutches again.

"Take care of yourself, Sarah. And can you flip the sign for me? Close enough to opening time now."

"Sure enough. Have a good day."

I flipped the sign, shoved open the door, and stepped on to a bustling sidewalk, accompanied by the roar of a Tyrannosaurus Rex.

10

It was going to be a busy day.

First Tetris, then Tracy and Tabitha, had promised to meet me at Angie's to go over a plan. Delta Crabbit and Preston, too. I'd invited Uncle Cyrus, but he'd been noncommittal.

I also had to get to Cecilia's to meet with Toby and the sprites, and sandwich in time to do the actual job that kept Rhiannon in kibble. All without being able to drive. If I could brake without using my foot, things would've been fine. But as it was? Stefon insisted on driving me around. Though considering he makes four times as much money as I do, I hated to take him away from his work.

By the time I navigated across the road—using the crosswalk and light for once—and pushed my way into the Blueberry Café, the gang was already gathered, including Jerry and Ash. I gave them all a quick wave, then crutched past the big community bulletin board and headed for the counter.

"I'm beginning to think you like my muffins," Angie

said, voice dry. Wisps of blond hair escaped from her blue kerchief. Buster pushed through the swinging kitchen door, carrying a fresh tray of scones. His face glistened with sweat. He slammed the tray on the steel work counter behind Angie and practically flung himself back into the kitchen.

Okay. What's up with you, buddy?

"Buster seems a bit grouchy. Hot in the kitchen today?"

Angie exhaled dramatically. "Baking in August is always a steam bath. At least we're not inland. I don't think I could take doing this job in Portland. But he's miffed because I told him he couldn't have a raise until he'd been here at least six months."

She glanced at the two people queued up behind me. When had they come in? Usually, I maintained better awareness of my surroundings. My witchy senses were scrambled, and I needed to do something about that. Stat. But for now...

"Blueberry muffin and English Breakfast tea, please. I'll send one of the teens up to get my order when its ready."

"Thanks, Sarah."

She'd already turned to help the next person in line, so I navigated between tables toward the back where two tables were smooshed together, creating one large obstacle at the edge of the main dining area. The place was full. Still part of the breakfast rush, but it was the only time all of us could meet at once.

Tabitha leapt up to pull out a chair for me, as Tracy took my crutches. I eased myself into the chair with a sigh of relief.

"How are you, dear?" asked Delta Crabbit. The witch's

hair was almost tame today. She must not have started stressing out yet.

"I feel like a whiner, but I'm already sick of this. I've got so much to do today—along with the bookstore—and too many things require a car."

"I'm happy to drive you," Delta replied. "Preston and I."

That was astonishing.

"You have a car?"

I only ever saw Delta walking and wasn't sure I trusted her behind the wheel.

"I do. It's garaged most of the time, but I do have one…" She sounded less certain now. That did not set my mind at ease.

Luckily, Tracy chimed in.

"My mom said to tell you that since it's her slow season, she'd be happy to drive you around. She said, quote, 'I'm driving you two hither and yon, so I may as well help Sarah, too.'"

"She said that?" I asked, just as Angie rang a bell and called out my name.

"Yeah," Tabitha replied, shoving back her chair. "I was there. Carol actually said 'hither and yon.' I'll get your order."

Tears pricked threateningly at the corners of my eyes. I was touched by everyone's offers of help. While Dad was dying, I'd grown used to doing it all by myself. Even after Cecilia moved back to town and I started dating Stefon… well. I guess old habits die slowly, don't they?

But you're a witch, Sarah, and witches know how to change.

That thought came directly from my inner wisdom, or higher self, or whatever you want to call it. And yes, one of

the definitions of magic is "the art of changing conscious-
ness at will." Guess I needed to get on that.

"I brought my cards," Jerry Hamamoto said, shoving
his tortoiseshell glasses higher onto the narrow bridge of
his nose. "Figured a little reading might help shed more
light on the situation."

He began to shuffle, though even from across the
table, I could tell it wasn't his usual deck.

"What cards are those?" I asked.

"The Faeries Oracle," he replied. "They wanted to
come along today."

Huh. Magical objects were like that. Sometimes they
were clear. Insistent even.

I noticed his son, Ash, sitting quietly next to him,
wearing some sort of anime T-shirt, small glass of orange
juice and a half-decimated cinnamon-swirl muffin in front
of him. He looked troubled.

"Everything okay there, Ash?"

He shook his head, one dark lock falling over his
forehead.

"I'm worried about the sprites."

"Why is that?"

He looked up at me with liquid dark eyes, looking so
sorrowful I wanted to hug him.

"If someone is stealing faery dust, won't that hurt
them?"

His dad glanced down at the card on the bottom of the
deck, frowned, and resumed shuffling. "It could, sweet-
heart. It could start to change their magic."

"Why would someone do that?"

I shared a glance with Jerry, who gave a slight shake of
his head. Okay then. We weren't going to talk about drugs,
or power, or any of the rest of it.

"Some people are greedy," I temporized. "They see that someone else has something and they want it for themselves."

Jerry gave me a thankful smile, then started laying out the cards in a simple Elemental pattern on a cleared part of the table.

Tabitha set down my tea and muffin.

"Thank you!"

"I saw something!" Delta burst out.

"What?" I asked, almost spitting out my first mouthful of tea.

Delta began tugging on her hair, and Preston bounced on the chair next to her, purple cap bobbing up and down.

"We saw some people and dogs!" the gnome shouted, though luckily, being a gnome, his voice wasn't loud enough to carry past the hubbub of the milk steamer, people's conversation, and the Guns N' Roses currently gracing the café sound system.

"I don't get it," Tracy said, pausing with a bite of scone halfway to her mouth. "There are a lot of dogs around. Everyone's prepping for Wag a Lot."

Delta pressed a finger to the side of her nose. One of those, *Ah, but I know something you don't know* gestures that I've never understood.

"What Preston did not say is that one of those people was not human." She looked triumphant.

Jerry looked up from his cards. "That's what these are telling me."

"What?" Now it was my turn to be confused. I looked across the table at the unusual deck, with its painted images of strange fae creatures.

The rest of us looked from Delta to Jerry and back again.

Tabitha set her coffee mug down with a *thunk*. Was it okay for a girl her age to be drinking coffee? Something I'd ask her parents if I ever met them.

"Isn't somebody going to tell us what the heck you're talking about?"

"Delta?" I asked.

"You tell them," she said, pointing to Mr. Hamamoto.

But it was Ash, peering intently at the cards, who answered.

"It's a grig."

"A grig?" I'd never even heard of such a creature. Ash slid the card across the table so I could see.

It was done in Brian Froud's inimitable flowing style and showed a small fae creature with a large overbite grin, pointed ears, and a floppy hat. Its face reminded me slightly of a Commedia Dell'arte mask from the Ren Faire.

"The card says, 'Mickle a Muckle,' not grig."

Ash was such a good kid; he didn't even roll his eyes at me. But I could feel it.

"That's this one's name. You know, like Sarah. But it's a grig."

"Yes," said Preston, almost touching the card with his little button nose. "What we saw most certainly looked like this fellow. Hmm...a grig..."

He stroked his chin with one chubby hand.

"I'll bite," said Tracy. "What's a grig?"

Jerry pulled out the reference book that came with the cards—he never needed one for regular Tarot, but oracle cards were different—and scanned a couple of pages.

"Says here that grigs are playful and silly fae creatures and are slightly larger than gnomes...but that Mickle a Muckle name? It literally means 'mixed blessing.'"

Great. Just great. I had no idea why a grig would have

appeared in town. And what did they have to do with Carlson's disappearance, and the stolen faery dust?

I was once again out of my magical depth. Why couldn't I just run my bookshop and dance under the full moon? Why did I have to...

Delta jabbed me with a pointy finger.

"Ouch! Why'd you do that?"

"You were drifting. And we need to know what's next."

I sat back, thinking, then looked up at the ceiling.

"Uncle Cyrus, we're going to need your help again." Hopefully he'd hear me and pop by. Or I'd need to text him, which he hated for some reason. Said it interfered with his vibrations. But whatever, if he didn't show up again soon, he'd need to deal. Because I might have been magical Justice in Seashell Cove, but all that really meant?

Was that I knew how to ask for help when I needed it.

And with a missing surfer, stolen faery dust, and one happy-go-lucky, possibly thieving grig? We were going to need it.

11

Carol stopped by the store to arrange driving me on some of my errands when my shift was through. She was leaning on the counter, smelling of sunscreen and lemon shampoo.

"Is it just me, or is this town getting stranger and stranger?" I asked.

Rhiannon hacked out a laugh. Carol looked alarmed.

"Is she going to cough up a hairball?"

"I don't think so," I said, narrowing my eyes in warning. Rhiannon just blinked and went back to washing herself on the front counter.

Carol's gaze lingered on Rhiannon for a moment, then she shook her blond hair.

"It's not just you. There's definitely more paranormal activity, as the civilians call it."

I slumped onto the high stool behind the counter, keeping an eye out for customers. Luckily most people seemed happy enough to browse and weren't needing immediate attention. The teenagers were back in the occult section looking up faery dust and grigs.

"I mean, I've never had to deal with most of these things," I said. "First it was the centaurs, now grigs, and who knows what else and oh!" I snapped my fingers. "I completely forgot."

"Forgot what?" Carol asked, thumbing through a display of handmade greeting cards as we talked.

"Gargoyles."

She paused and looked around.

"Gargoyles? Like, stone decorations? What do they have to do with anything?"

"There was a gargoyle in the shop. I scared it, and it disappeared."

"Really? The shop has a gargoyle?" She peered down the back aisle as if trying to find it.

"I didn't think it did. But it was there. I forgot about it after I hurt my ankle."

There was a clatter of books and the sound of rapidly walking sneakers. The teens appeared from between two bookcases, each holding a book

"What did you find out?" I asked.

"Faery dust helps the smaller fae to fly. And it can spread magic to other beings, too," Tracy said.

Huh. Okay. No wonder the sprites were upset. If they lost their ability to fly because of this, that would spell bigger trouble than I'd even feared. It's like any small environmental change—you never know the ramifications of one small change. Sprites not flying? And faery magic spreading? Who knows what might happen?

"And grigs?" Carol asked.

"Grigs definitely seem to just want people to be happy," Tabitha replied.

"So why the 'mixed blessing'?" I mused.

::*All faeries are a mixed blessing*,:: Rhiannon said,

pausing in the middle of licking her front paws. *::As a matter of fact....::*

I tried to tune out the cat's voice in my head, but still heard the word "obnoxious" quite clearly.

Tabitha tapped a finger to her lips. "I think it's because what a grig thinks will make you happy, and what you think will make you happy, aren't always the same thing."

"Or maybe you think it will make you happy, but it can actually hurt you," Carol said. "Like eating a whole chocolate cake instead of one piece. Or drinking too much alcohol."

Great. Why did magic—and life—have to be so dang complex?

"Put it all on the list, please. And thanks, you two. Great work."

They beamed at me.

"While you're at the research," I said, "could you also look up gargoyles?"

"Oh, yeah, you know, we were going to ask you about the new statue," Tabitha said.

"Where did you get it? It's really cute," Tracy said.

"Wait, the gargoyle is back?"

"What do you mean?" Tabitha asked. "You don't think it's real, do you?"

"Let's head back and I'll explain. Can you grab Duncan, please?" I said to Tracy, "then meet us back in Biff's corner."

Carol and Tabitha forged ahead, slipping easily among the warren of bookshelves and browsers.

Moving more slowly, I crutched my way through the stacks, greeting customers, pointing out a book or two, and offering a couple of recommendations. Rhiannon was with me, so people had to greet her as well.

Finally, after what seemed an enormously long amount of time, I reached the back corner of the store. And sure enough, on the shelf near the corner chair was that gargoyle with the stone bow on its head.

"You," I said.

Its eyes grew wide and it sniffed, then froze. Playing statues.

"You don't fool me," I said. "I see you. I know you're real. And don't even think of disappearing again."

I laid a hand on its shoulder. It gasped.

"What do you want from me? I didn't do anything. I'm not hurting anything."

The poor thing sounded panicked.

"I didn't say you were." I kept my voice calm and reasonable. "But I do need to know why you're here and what you want."

I heard Tracy and Tabitha whispering at each other.

Carol stood beside me.

"Let me," she said reaching out.

I shrugged and removed my hand, but before my fingers left the stone shoulder I felt the gargoyle start to shift.

"Oh no you don't." I gripped tighter.

"Carol?"

She put her hand on the other shoulder.

"Got it?" I gently removed mine. The gargoyle stabilized again.

Rhiannon paced on the floor in front of the bookcase. She seemed agitated, but I didn't have time to ask why. I needed to keep my attention on the stone creature in front of me.

"We don't want to hurt you. We're friends. Okay?" I held out my hands in what I hoped was a gentle and placating fashion. But since I've never met a gargoyle, I couldn't tell how it would respond.

Luckily, it seemed to calm them. And I also had a feeling Carol was boosting a little calming energy through the hand still touching the gargoyle's shoulder.

I hoped the teens were making note of the fact that touching a gargoyle seems to anchor it in space and time. I would need to ask Cyrus about that. Hmm, maybe I could even practice on him. See what happened next time he wanted to pop in or out.

Rhiannon sneezed. Tracy stepped forward and scratched Rhiannon's head, then looked up at the gargoyle.

"Can you tell us why you're here?" Tracy's voice was gentler than mine. The gargoyle looked down, turning those big, liquid eyes on her.

Don't ask me how stone eyes can be liquid. They just are.

"I...I needed to get away," it said. "I was scared. And I was told this was a safe place to be."

It hiccupped, and, wonder of wonders, Rhiannon leapt up on the shelf beside it, and pressed her little body against the gargoyle's stone back. That seemed to calm the creature even more than whatever Carol was pumping out.

Another note to self: cats have a soothing effect on gargoyles. When they choose to.

"And?" Tabitha asked.

"And Biff has been so nice to me. The nicest anyone's been in a long time..." The gargoyle burst into tears again.

Sarah, do not roll your eyes.

I took a calming breath, braced myself on my crutches, and put as benign and kindly a look on my face as I could.

"Well, whoever told you that was right," I said. "You are welcome here as long as, you know, you don't do any damage. Speaking of which, was it you that knocked the books off the shelf?"

The gargoyle's eyes grew wide again, but Rhiannon pressed harder, and nudged the gargoyle with her nose. It calmed again.

"I didn't mean to," it said. "I was just looking. But I heard someone coming in. I got scared."

That someone was me.

"Scottish castles?" I asked.

The gargoyle shrugged, and Carol slowly removed her hand.

The gargoyle seemed more solid and willing to stay now. Despite the stone tears still running down its face. Rhiannon began to purr.

Wow. Rhiannon almost never purrs. Cats must *really* like gargoyles.

"I...I had ancestors from Scotland, and I like castles. All gargoyles like old stone buildings."

Well, that made sense.

"And the puppy book?"

"I like dogs, too."

Rhiannon looked offended.

"And cats!" the gargoyle hurried to add. "I've always wanted a dog..."

Rhiannon hissed.

"...or a cat! You know. A companion. But I've never been able to. Most warm-blooded animals don't want to live on top of buildings."

Go figure. A gargoyle who liked puppies. I was learning so many new things. But I kept getting distracted. And that wasn't usual either. It made me wonder if that was part of what was going on with the stolen faery dust and our missing surfer.

"Who are you running from?" Tracy asked, then looked at me and pointed toward the comfy chair in the corner.

Bossy. But a good idea. I really needed to sit down and stop looming over the gargoyle. I eased my way down into the cozy chair and let my crutches drop to the floor.

"Who are you running from?" Tracy repeated herself. "And how can we help?"

"And what happened to your building?" Tabitha asked.

Good question.

"My building got knocked down last year, and some people took me in. Told me I had a home with them. But then they started using me. Making me carry things. And they were hurting people. And I didn't like it. It didn't feel safe." The gargoyle's voice dropped near the end until I had to lean to catch the gravelly whisper.

"Were they stealing from the sprites?" I asked.

The gargoyle gasped and *poof* disappeared. Again.

Rhiannon's furry head whipped around, startled. Then she leapt off the bookcase and sauntered back toward the front as if nothing had happened.

Cats.

Tracy looked at me. "Really, Sarah?"

"How was I supposed to know that would make the gargoyle disappear? But at least we have another piece of the puzzle now."

"Really?" Carol asked. "And what's that?"

"We figured out that it's bigger than just a missing surfer. Bigger even than the stolen faery dust. As a matter of fact, it sounds like a drug ring to me."

Tabitha scrunched her adolescent-smooth brow. "I don't get it. How do you figure?"

"Clearly you need to start reading more thrillers," I said. "Half the time when something goes wrong like this? Drug ring. And it sounds like whoever it is was using the gargoyle as some sort of mule."

And that was the last thing Seashell Cove needed.

12

The Seashell Cove shelter was too busy dealing with animal intake and adoptions to actually organize the Wag a Lot volunteer signups, so The Historic Kelpie had offered to take on that duty. As a result, Carol dropped me in front of the brightly colored whale and kraken mural and went on her way.

I crutched my way to the through the courtyard, past the old, dry-docked boat and the family suites housed in long, low slung 1950s era buildings. The courtyard was dotted with fanciful, ocean-themed sculptures. On days when I had time, I always tried to spot what was new. Today was not that day. It took all my effort to reach the front porch of the main house of the inn. An old three-story building, this main part of the Kelpie was built in the 1920s. On the porch sat a long, life-sized shark with a saddle on its back. Tourists love to sit on the shark and send photos home and post on social media.

I opened the doors and was greeted as usual by the smell of popcorn and the sound of a retro film playing on an ancient television.

The boxy TV was wall mounted over the big popcorn machine and today's movie selection was *The Thin Man*. William Powell drinking far too many martinis and generally being a hilarious cutup. I grinned at their antics as I passed through the tiny 1940s era lobby and into the dimly lit bar. Every local knew that if you couldn't find anyone in the Kelpie lobby, you headed to the kitchen. That was Liam's favorite place. He had owned the building for a few decades and was the one responsible for all of the wacky art crowding its walls and even the dining room ceiling.

The spacious room had booths lining the walls beneath windows overlooking a small courtyard, and a long communal table in the center. Liam was there, one hand in his salt-and-pepper hair, staring at a laptop screen and tapping away on a calculator. He sat in on of the dozen mismatched chairs surrounding the twelve-foot-long expanse of wood.

An old-fashioned phone booth crouched in the corner and up above, a mannequin in a sailor suit piloted a dinghy. The historic inn was affectionately known by many of us as the Haunted Kelpie because, well, it had a lot of ghosts. Some of them were now my friends, which you might not think was strange, but I was still getting used to it. Being both a Justice and a witch has its perks and drawbacks. I wasn't yet sure which exactly the ghosts were. A bit of both, I suppose.

"Sarah," Liam said, looking up from his calculator and a stack of receipts. An old-timey ledger—the hardcover kind with leather corners—sat on the table next to the shiny new laptop.

"You do your books the old-fashioned way? Hmm..." I said, crutching my way forward. He leaped to his feet and pulled out a chair.

"Yeah. I like to have paper backup for everything. Just in case." He pulled up a padded bench from the end of one of the booths. I angled my chair and raised my feet up in relief.

"I heard about your accident. How's the ankle?"

"It's getting better, but I won't be well enough to do the run. So, I wanted to see if there were any volunteer slots left."

"Oh, that'd be grand," he said. "I've got the signup sheets in the bar."

He rushed off to get them, returning with a clipboard bristling with papers.

"What would you like to do?" He scanned the top paper. "Give out dog treats? Water or sports drinks for the humans? Corral the children?"

"Something simple," I said. "And something that won't take all day."

"Dog treat duty before the race it is, then."

I looked around. "How are things going here?"

"Well enough. Ghosts have been relatively quiet, which is good, and we're booked solid for Wag a Lot. And then next month we have a lot of bookings for Find a Float."

Every September, Seashell Cove commissions local glassblowers to design and make elaborate fishing floats. Volunteers plant them throughout the beach and the cliffs for tourists in one large scavenger hunt. It's very popular. I avoided the beach like the plague while it was going on, but appreciate the extra business it brings in.

I scratched my name down under the Dog Treats heading on the roster and added my email and phone number. Liam was giving me a look.

"If I didn't know better, because of course you'd tell me

if there was trouble," he said, "I'd think there was something more wrong than just your ankle."

I sighed, blowing a hair off my face.

"Well... There is the man who caused my fall. He's missing, and I've got Tetris taking care of his dog. And well, this is strange..."

"Sarah, I've lived in Seashell Cove for decades. And I know you and knew your father before you. I'm okay with a little strange. Besides..." He tilted his head at the ceiling, where two floors up an old, abandoned speakeasy still threw parties for all the resident ghosts and their friends.

I nodded. He had a point about that.

"Okay," I said. "There are two things. What do you know about gargoyles? And have you ever heard of a grig? Small. Cheerful. Overbite? Long nose and pointed ears?"

I described what I remembered of the Faeries' Oracle card as best I could.

He rubbed his chin thoughtfully, and smiled, blue eyes thoughtful. "Gargoyles belong on buildings. I know that much. And grigs? They're some sort of fae creature, I imagine. At least it sounds that way...."

I nodded in what I hoped was an encouraging fashion.

But Liam's thoughtful smile turned into a frown. "But even my sainted great-granny from Ireland never talked about grigs, so I'm afraid I can't help you."

"Dang."

I knew it was a long shot, but I had hoped he would know something. I was grasping at straws. This investigation was headed nowhere, faster than I could currently run.

There was a clattering in the lobby, and then the sound of someone running and panting through the bar.

Sophie, bottle-red hair flying, burst into the dining room, eyes panicked, pale cheeks flushed with effort.

"Sophie?" Liam pushed his chair back and rose.

The inn's cleaning person braced herself against the door jamb and held up a hand, signaling that she needed to catch her breath. Her ample chest heaved beneath her Historic Kelpie Inn T-shirt. The horse cresting the wave on the logo looked as if it was galloping.

After around thirty seconds that felt like an age, she straightened.

"A man just collapsed in the front courtyard. He's raving about...I don't even know what. Can you come?"

Liam was already heading past her. I grabbed my crutches and did my best to follow Sophie, though after a day on crutches, my armpits were seriously sore.

By the time I made it out front, Sophie and Liam already had the man propped on a bench. And I recognized him. All too well.

I crutched faster.

"Carlson! Where have you been? Are you okay?"

"Duuudde," he groaned. "I think I'm gonna be sick."

I stopped where I was, and Liam and Sophie both stepped back.

We all watched in horrified fascination as Carlson slowly swayed on the bench. Forward. Then back. Then forward again. One hand clutched his stomach area, and the other was cupped over his mouth.

Finally, he stopped and we all breathed a sigh of relief.

"Can you stand?" Liam asked.

"Think so."

Liam helped Carlson to his feet. The surfer looked a bit greenish beneath his tan. Sophie ran ahead to open the front door.

"If you can manage one short flight of stairs, we can get you comfortable on a sofa in the lounge. And I think a nice cup of mint tea is in order."

"Sounds great, dude. Thanks."

Carlson allowed himself to be led, leaning heavily on Liam.

My head swam with questions. Where had Carlson gone? How had he suddenly reappeared? Why hadn't he asked after Board Wax yet? What had made him so ill?

And how the heck was I going to get up that flight of stairs?

Liam laboriously helped Carlson up the stairway as Sophie headed off to the kitchen to make tea.

I texted Stefon.

He was set to fetch me for dinner with Uncle Cyrus soon, anyway, so I knew he'd be about to close down whatever he was working on for the day.

Minutes later, he stalked into the lobby where I was ensconced on an overstuffed horsehair loveseat, an ice bag on my ankle—courtesy of Sophie—watching *The Thin Man*. My shoes were on the floor, next to my crutches.

I say lobby, but really the entrance to the haunted inn is little more than an entry hall, with a few books and postcards, the popcorn machine, and ancient television with—I kid you not—a VCR. Movie posters plaster the walls from the ceiling to the threadbare baroque carpet.

All of that is to say: my large dark knight of a boyfriend filled the place. Deliciously.

"Babe. Why exactly do you need to get up the stairs when there's this perfectly good loveseat right here?"

He leaned down to kiss me, his curly beard tickling my cheeks. His lips were warm, and he tasted of coffee and sugar.

"I told you," I said, when we finally broke apart. "Liam has Carlson upstairs. There's no room for anyone down here, and Carlson really needed to lie down. He looked like he was going to puke."

Stefon sighed, pretending to be put upon, but the edges of a grin snuck through. "And I suppose you want me to carry you?"

"No, just help…"

And then his arms were around me and he was scooping me toward his big belly and broad chest.

I yelped and the ice bag went tumbling to the carpet.

"My ice bag! And crutches!"

"I'll get them in a minute."

And then I was bobbing along like a cork in the ocean as Stefon carried me up the stairs, taking care at the one switchback so I didn't bang my ankle on the railing.

Told you he's a knight, even when he's not wearing armor.

13

You know, Cecilia and I made a great couple, but she's a lot smaller than me. When a size-sixteen person needs to be carried upstairs? A larger, stronger human is useful.

"Hey Liam," Stefon said when we reached the lounge of the inn. "Special delivery."

"Stefon, my man!" The proprietor once again leapt to his feet. "Sarah, do you prefer a couch, or a chair and ottoman?"

I would have loved a couch. To take a long nap. But that was not in the cards.

"Chair, please."

Liam dragged an ottoman over toward a gorgeous leather club chair, and Stefon plunked me down. Gently, of course, though I was not too graceful about it.

"Be right back," he said.

Carlson moaned from a couch across from me. A painting of an ancient mariner glared down at him with a baleful eye, as if disapproving whatever it was Carlson might or might not have done. I couldn't blame the sea captain, even though he could just as easily have been glaring my way. And had, in times past.

"We're just waiting on Sophie with the tea," Liam said. "I figured Carlson here could use a few moments to gather his wits."

Liam gave me a look that finished the sentence, *Before you start grilling him.*

I smiled placidly. "That's fine."

Then I looked around the room. Same club chairs. Same overstuffed sofas, coffee tables, bookshelves, fringed lamps, and same overabundance of seafaring artwork. Same ghostly staircase in the far corner, though not everyone could see it.

And, on the low bookcase right near the hallway leading to the bedroom suites, between a sea-green fish float and a hunk of white coral...a gargoyle crouched.

"Liam? Is that new?"

"Is what new?"

Stefon was back, followed by Sophie. He handed me the ice pack and set my crutches down on the floor before easing into a club chair himself. Sophie busied herself setting tea things on the low coffee table in the center of our little seating cluster.

I placed the ice on my ankle, and thanked Sophie for the mug of steaming mint tea. Settling into the club chair, I turned back to Liam, who now had his own mug in hand.

So far, Carlson hadn't said a word. But, out of it or not, that would need to change. Soon.

"The gargoyle," I said, then blew across the surface of the tea, giving myself a nice mint-scented steam facial while I was at it. I never had much time for proper skin care, so sometimes I take what I can get.

"What gargoyle? I don't have any..."

Liam set his mug on the coffee table and stalked over to the bookcase.

"How the heck did you get up here?"

I swear the gargoyle cringed, but that must have been my eyes playing tricks on me, because Liam picked it up and it sure just looked like a hunk of garden statuary to me.

Liam frowned. "This showed up on the front porch a couple of days ago, and I set it out in the back garden with the other sculptures. I have no idea how it got up here. Sophie?"

The housekeeper shook her fading red locks. "Never seen it before. It wasn't here last time I dusted."

Sophie's voice sounds like she smoked too many cigarettes and drank one too many whiskeys, though I know for a fact she's one of Seashell Cove's middle-aged health nuts. It's all granola and kombucha for her, at least these days.

Not only was my ankle throbbing again, I was a bit cranky that not only did we need to question Carlson, but now there was a spare gargoyle to deal with as well.

And I didn't trust the gargoyles, particularly not one I'd never spoken to. Until I knew what, if anything, they had to do with faery dust or Carlson and his disappearance, I didn't really want a gargoyle to be privy to this conversation.

On the other, *other* hand, I didn't want to take my eyes off the creature in case it disappeared.

Liam moved to set the gargoyle down on the shelf.

"Wait," I called. "Keep your hands on it!"

"What? What are you talking about?" He hefted the

gargoyle. "It's just a statue. Sure, we don't know where it came from, but..."

I shook my head. "Just trust me on this, will you?" I turned to Stefon. "Do you think you can keep a hold of it and cover its ears at the same time?"

He gave me one of those *What are you up to now?* looks. When I didn't say "Haha, just kidding!" he sighed and turned back to Liam.

"Can you hand me that thing?"

Liam did, then sat back down.

Stefon gripped the gargoyle against his belly then turn to Sophie.

"Got any clean hand towels lying around?"

"Sure do." Sophie hoisted herself up and scurried down the hallway, returning quickly with a small white towel which Stefon fashioned into a makeshift turban, covering the gargoyle's ears. It looked ridiculous.

I swore the gargoyle frowned, and yep, sure enough, it shook its head, trying to loosen the towel.

Stefon clamped his hands over the gargoyle's ears.

"Whoa." Carlson finally spoke. "Did that statue just shake its head? Dude."

"Welcome back to the land of the living," Liam said. "Care to tell us how you ended up in the courtyard of my inn?"

I relaxed a bit. It's always nice when someone else takes bad cop.

Carlson looked confused and scratched the stubble on his chin.

"That's where I am? The inn?" He shoved up onto his elbows, looking around with interest. "Hey. I heard this place is haunted. Are there really ghosts?"

"We don't have time for that," I snapped out. So much

for good cop. "I need to find out where you've been, why you abandoned Board Wax, and what you have to do with the gargoyles and missing faery dust."

Carlson's eyebrows shot up towards his hairline.

"Oh, dude! Board Wax! Is Board Wax okay?"

"Board Wax is fine, no thanks to you." I crossed my arms over my chest. "And my ankle sucks."

Liam held up a placating hand, but Sophie settled deeper into her chair, looking as if she wished she'd brought up some popcorn to munch while she watched the show. I didn't blame her. The Kelpie popcorn was top notch.

My stomach growled.

"We'll be at dinner soon," Stefon whispered, and patted my thigh with one big hand before clamping it back over the gargoyle's towel-covered ear.

"Tell us what you remember," I said. "What happened after you almost brained me with the Frisbee? Before you disappeared."

Now it was Carlson's turn to look panicked. His eyes darted from me to Liam to Sophie to Stefon with the realization that while he might be safe for the moment, he was also trapped.

"I didn't do anything!"

"I think you did," I replied. "I think you were dealing faery dust."

"Is that what it was? Dang. Dude just told me it was happy powder."

"And you thought that was better?" Sophie chimed in.

Good point.

He shrugged. "You know, dude, it's none of my business what people want to put in their bodies. As long as it doesn't hurt anyone."

"How do you know it doesn't hurt anyone?" Now Stefon was pissed.

"You wait just a minute!" Liam's pale Irish face going from red to purple as he glared at the surfer.

"You can't be dealing unknown substances in our town. Especially not during tourist season! Happy dust!" Liam spat out. "If you didn't know what was in the packets, there was no way you should have been selling them!"

Liam's finger jabbed towards Carlson as if it were a knife. The surfer scooted as far back on the sofa as he could, trying to get away from Liam. The proprietor leaned toward him, jabbing, about ready to spring from his chair.

"Let's all just calm down a moment," Stefon said. His tone was reasonable, but his voice also made it clear he would brook no argument. I alternately call that his Knight of the Realm voice or his Dungeon Master voice. Amazingly, it works. I keep telling him that's his own form of magic.

Everyone obeyed. Even me. We all took a breath and relaxed ever so slightly. Including the gargoyle. It frankly looked pretty comfy nestled there in Stefon's lap despite the towel and the hands over its ears. I didn't blame the gargoyle. I was always pretty comfy in Stefon's lap myself.

"Carlson," I said, "clearly, you're in trouble. And clearly no one's coming to help you if you ended up dazed and confused in the courtyard of the inn, so you may as well just tell us what you know."

"Dude." He looked at Sophie. "Can I have some more of this tea?"

Now I wanted to throttle him but forced myself to sit still as Sophie replenished our cups.

"Thank you, Sophie." I said. "Carlson?"

"Well, it's like this, dude. I was at that market thing, just before sunset..."

"The Saturday Craft Fair?" Sophie asked. That was a new thing the town was trying out to boost local artisans and bring more cash and interest to Seashell Cove. If it did well, they were thinking of adding a holiday fair come winter.

"Yeah. I guess so. But you know, I was out there looking around. Stuff looked cool. I stopped to look at some gnarly statues. Like that one." He jerked his chin toward the swaddled gargoyle. "And the dude, said his name was Stuart, said I looked cool. Did I want to earn some extra cash? Easy money."

Now Stefon was looking grim again. We were taking it in turns wanting to choke our errant surfer.

"And you agreed," Stefon growled.

Carlson blanched. "Yeah. It was dumb. I know, dude! But I'm *stuck* here, sleeping in my truck. I ran out of money. My truck broke down. I need the cash to fix it so I can be on my way. I just wasn't sure what else to do."

And, wonder of wonders, Carlson the surfer burst into tears.

"And now I don't even have my dog," he sobbed.

"Board Wax is being very well taken care of," I said to Carlson. "He'll be happy to see you whenever you're ready."

And as soon as we figure out for sure you're not helping out this Stuart guy anymore. Though that didn't seem likely, considering Carlson had been dumped in Liam's courtyard and was clearly distressed.

But for all I knew, the surfer was a world class actor. Regardless, it was clear we weren't going to get any more out of Carlson for now.

I sighed, and muttered to Stefon, "Can we go to dinner now?"

Liam looked slightly abashed.

"You can stay here, mate," he said. "We have a room open for a few days. Cancellation. But you'll have to work for it."

"I will!" Carlson said, swinging his legs to the floor and sitting up. "I promise."

"This conversation isn't over," I said. "We'll be back."

I turned to Stefon, who stood in readiness, looming in the overstuffed room.

"I'm afraid we're going to have to take the gargoyle."

"Of course, we are."

He set the gargoyle in my lap, gave its head a pat, then bent to pick me up again.

"Toodle-oo." I waved my fingers at the assembled crew, then clutched the statue. Stefon was on the move.

But a strange look had passed across Carlson's face.

Later, I would wish I'd stopped to ask him why.

14

After dinner at Costa's with Uncle Cyrus, we all headed to Toby and Cecilia's garden. One nice thing about summer at this latitude was the extended daylight. which made doing all the things much easier. Of course, it also meant I wanted to be home by the fire at four p.m. during the winter months.

The only unfortunate thing about the appointment with Toby is that we missed out on sunset over the water, which is frankly my favorite reason to go to Seashell Cove's most expensive restaurant.

Especially on Uncle Cyrus's dime.

But here we were in Toby and Cecilia's garden on a small deck area the hob and my best friend had built earlier in the summer. Cyrus and Stefon sat in chairs, with the gargoyle on Stefon's lap again. I really didn't want to leave it alone and risk it disappearing. Cecilia sat on a lovely garden bench, and me? On a lounge chair that elevated my ankle quite nicely.

It was a pleasant evening here, surrounded by the gentle smell of herbs and growing vegetables, buzzing sprites and bumblebees, and all manner of beautiful flowers whose names I couldn't begin to tell you.

What can I say? Mostly I'm an indoors, book-reading kind of person. If you don't count jogging on the beach, which I wouldn't be doing anytime soon. And that was starting to nag at me. I really needed to run.

Jogging is my one main physical outlet, and it calms my mind more than anything else.

"You just better hurry up and heal," I said to my ankle.

"You okay, babe?" Stefon asked.

"I'm fine. Thanks." I squeezed his hand, grateful for our deepening relationship. Neither of us had explicitly mentioned moving in together, but I could tell we'd both been thinking about it. Trouble was, neither of us wanted to give up our current homes.

Toby bustled about in what I'd come to call their "garden-colored" clothing. Green canvas pants and brown T-shirt just a couple of shades darker than Toby's skin. They poured iced lemonade into tall glasses. I took a sip.

"Mmm..." The tart and sweet lemony combination was flavored with mint Toby grew in this very garden. Toby handed me a plate of small cookies.

"Baked this morning. Before it got too hot," they said.

"Must be nice living with a hob," I said to Cecilia, and not for the first time.

She grinned and stuffed a cookie in her mouth.

"Yeah, it's pretty great. Not that I don't love you, Sarah. But you're no great shakes in the kitchen."

Didn't I know it?

"I love you anyway," Stefon said.

"Besides," he said to Cecilia, "I like to cook myself."

"And one cook in a relationship is plenty," I shot back.

Uncle Cyrus cleared his throat, interrupting our

banter. Toby sat next to Cecilia and gave a high whistle. Two of the sprites I had met before settled on the back of the extra chair Toby had set out for them.

One was golden. The other green. Both were as beautiful as butterflies or dragonflies or any of those other winged insects you saw around gardens or ponds. I'm sure Toby knew the insects by name, too, every last one of them.

The green one glared at Stefon's lap. That was Rowena, who seemed to be some sort of leader among the sprites in Toby's garden.

"What's that doing here?"

Huh. I guess sprites and gargoyles didn't much get along.

"It was at The Historic Kelpie," I said. "And I think it has something to do with this case."

And since one gargoyle had appeared in my bookshop, and this one had appeared out of nowhere, we needed to figure out the connection. So much so that I'd decided letting the gargoyle in on our conversations would be more useful than keeping its ears covered.

Call it witch's intuition if you want. Or maybe I just didn't think Stefon would be okay with gargoyle-sitter duty if he wasn't invited to the meeting.

The golden sprite sniffed.

"Gargoyles always have something to do with *everything*."

"They're no good," said Rowena. Her green wings definitely were not as shiny as last time I'd seen the sprites. "And we don't trust them."

"Now wait a minute," I said, "let's not be hasty and jump to conclusions."

I had to say that as a Justice, even though I didn't yet

trust the gargoyles myself.

The gargoyle turned its head towards Stefon's chest, but said nothing. That seemed a little strange to me, that it had calmed down and no longer wanted to escape. But for all I knew, it was just biding its time. It seemed to like Stefon though. Which was a good thing.

"So," I said after taking another sip of delicious mint lemonade, "faery dust."

Both sprites fluttered their wings angrily, buzzing like beetles. Was it my imagination, or did they seem slower than usual?

"They stole it! And they've been stealing it!"

"I understand that," I said. "What I don't understand is how you collect the stuff, and how whoever it is got a hold of it. And did you see them?"

It was all a mystery to me. The sprites looked at each other.

Rowena tilted her tiny, sharp chin. "We cannot answer questions about the dust. It is forbidden."

I lifted my hands. "Look. I don't want to know your sprite secrets. I don't want to steal your faery dust. I know it's important to you. I just want to make this stop, so it doesn't happen anymore. And to do that, we need a lot more information. Like who 'they' are."

The green sprite flew back and forth, looking like a peripatetic hummingbird. Maybe that's how angry sprites think. Like a human paces.

I took the time to bite into a cookie. Buttery, lemony shortbread bliss.

"Oh, my Goddess! These are so good!"

Toby smiled, then ducked their head. I don't know if all hobs are shy, but Toby certainly is.

Cecilia ruffled their dark hair affectionately. Toby

grabbed her hand and kissed her palm. I stuffed another cookie in my mouth. So. Good.

Finally, Rowena settled on the chair back once again, green wings slightly drooping.

"We keep our store of faery dust in a hawthorn chest, bound with a silver chain."

"Sounds like something out of a D&D campaign," Stefon murmured beside me. Exactly.

"And where is this hawthorn chest?" Uncle Cyrus asked.

"We cannot tell you."

I gestured with my lemonade.

"Do you want our help or not?"

"We do, but..." The golden sprite shifted uncomfortably.

"But you are not used to talking about such things," Uncle Cyrus said. "And you were taught to trust no one. Magical or otherwise. I do not blame you."

His tone was reasonable, but he cheated a glance at me from the corner of his eyes before continuing. "But the Justice is correct. If we are to help you, we need as much information as possible. But let's leave that for now."

My eyes widened. Seriously, Cyrus?

He gave me a slight shake of his head and laced his fingers together. "Have either of you heard tell of a grig around these parts?"

Both sprites were off like a shot. Buzzing and humming, darting and diving.

I turned to Toby. "I take it they don't like grigs."

They lifted their shoulders and tilted their head as if to say *Who the heck knows with sprites?*

The sprites flew high in the air, and dive bombed the garden before flying upward again.

15

"How long is this going to take?" I asked, setting down my lemonade.

"When did you grow so impatient, Sarah?" Cecilia asked.

"Since I borked my ankle and a gargoyle showed up in my shop."

Stefon patted my shoulder.

"Not running makes her grumpy."

I fake-growled at him but had to admit he was right.

"I get that," Cecilia said. "I get grumpy if I don't get my car out on the open road for a stretch at least once a week, don't I, Toby?"

The hob smiled and nodded.

That made sense. In our own way, Cecilia and I both needed a sense of speed.

Finally, the sprites returned and perched on the chair back again.

"We don't like grigs," the green one—Rowena—said.

"I'm getting that impression," I said. "You don't like grigs, or gargoyles. Is it that you don't like creatures whose names start with G? Ghouls? Ghosts? Gremlins? Godzilla?"

The gold sprite tilted her tiny head at me as if trying to figure out whether I was mocking her. I kept my face placid.

Rowena looked as if she'd like to bite my thumb. But she just *hmphed*, and then spoke up.

"Grigs will tell you that they just want you to have a good time. But really, they are meddlers and mischief makers."

"Troublemakers!" the gold sprite said, stomping tiny feet. "Trouble, trouble, trouble!"

"And have you seen one around lately?" Cyrus asked.

"Yes."

My head snapped to the left so hard, I felt my neck crack. Because it wasn't a sprite that had spoken.

It was the gargoyle.

The stone creature shrank back against Stefon, who patted it reassuringly.

"It's okay, buddy," he said. "Tell us what you know."

The gargoyle cleared its throat and turned his big dark eyes Toby's way. "Might I trouble you for a spot of lemonade?"

Toby nodded and headed to the kitchen, returning with a tiny cup that he filled to the brim. The gargoyle drink thirstily.

"Thank you, kind being," it said. "The man was right about the market."

"What man?" Cecilia asked.

"Carlson," I replied. "Frisbee dude."

I turned back to the gargoyle. "That's who you mean, right? The surfer at the inn?"

The gargoyle nodded. "I know not whether he rides

the waves. But yes, the man at the inn. The troubled one. The one with the faery dust essence crowding his aura."

"Faery dust?" The green sprite shrieked, flying at the gargoyle's head. It ducked against Stefon's chest.

Rowena perched on Stefon's arm. Poor guy, he was getting to be a piece of magical creature furniture.

"What do you know?" she said. "Tell us. Tell us now."

The gargoyle shook its head. "Please," it moaned.

The green sprite rose back into the air, buzzing angrily.

"Say its name! We must get our revenge!"

Stefon spoke. "It might help if you let the gargoyle tell the story in its own time."

The green sprite settled again, this time on the arm of Stefon's chair as if it wanted to keep a close eye on the gargoyle.

"The grig acted as a scout, I think," the gargoyle said, "and the bad man was using us as lookouts."

"Bad man!" Rowena bristled. "The bad man stole our dust!"

"What man?" Uncle Cyrus asked.

"The bad man," the gargoyle repeated. "The man who captured us and makes us do such things as we do not wish to do. He said he wanted to 'show people a good time' but I do not think that was what he wanted at all."

And then the gargoyle burst into tears.

I looked at Uncle Cyrus. "Do all gargoyles cry a lot? Or just the only two I've met?"

He just looked at me, shaking his head, but he was smiling.

"Hey, buddy," Stefon said, leaning over the gargoyle. "It would really help if you could tell us more."

"He's traumatized," Toby said quietly. Toby's arms

were wrapped around their thin frame, and they were shaking. Cecilia leaned close, trying to comfort them.

"Toby?" I asked. "What do you know about this?"

The hob raised their deep brown eyes my way.

"I don't know anything," they said. "All I know is my friends are hurting and if they are hurt, then so am I."

That was such a powerful statement, it struck me to the core. That was what all of this Justice work was about, wasn't it? To help the ones who are hurting. It felt as if a puzzle piece slotted into place. When I looked away from Toby, Uncle Cyrus had his dark eyes fixed on me. We both smiled. He knew. He knew I had taken that in.

Even the sprites seemed calmer. It was as if all of us felt the impact of the hob's words.

"He is a very bad man." The gargoyle's rasping voice was so soft, each of us leaned in to listen more closely. "A bad man pretending to be good. And he kept his face in shadow, so we could not see who he was."

We waited. The gargoyle said nothing more. I sipped my lemonade. Though I couldn't see it from here, the sky showed the sun was westering toward the ocean horizon. It would be dark soon and the sprites were looking sleepy. They must bed down in full dark, heading to their nests or homes or tree hollows, or wherever it is that sprites live.

"Can you tell us anything more?" I asked. "About what this man wanted?"

The gargoyle shuddered, shaking its head.

"Money, I think. We didn't much care about that. But he promised us..."

I sat up straight.

"What did he promise?"

"He promised us a home. A permanent home. Not garden corners. Gargoyles hate garden corners when we're stuck there on the ground. We need to be up high. To fly like a kite. We need to See."

I could hear the capital letter on that last word but had no idea what it meant.

Uncle Cyrus spoke. "Gargoyles need height to tap your powers?"

The gargoyle nodded. "Yes! Yes! You understand!"

I was glad someone did. But there was still too much about this case that wasn't making a lick of sense.

A possum waddled into the garden, saw us, froze, and waddled back toward the fence. With the night creatures emerging, and the sprites drooping, and a traumatized gargoyle sitting on my boyfriend's lap? It was time to wrap things up.

"Let's call this meeting to a close. Thank you everyone. I need to sleep on this."

The sprites waved sleepily and headed off. The buzzing of their wings sounded far less angry now, which was a good thing.

Toby and Cecilia rose and started clearing the cookie plates and tea. Toby paused, the now-empty pitcher in their hands.

"Thank you, Sarah. I know we didn't get the answers we need, but it felt helpful all the same."

The hob headed through the door back into the kitchen, flicking on lights until the back of the house glowed.

"Will Toby be okay?" I asked.

Cecilia gazed at the kitchen window. "They'll be fine. Any kind of strife is hard on them, but we'll work it out."

She kissed my temple and headed in.

Cyrus looked out across the garden, deep in contemplation.

"Cyrus?"

He startled. "I can figure out why someone would steal faery dust to use in trade with other magical creatures. But I can't figure out why they would be selling it to human beings."

If only the gargoyle wasn't so traumatized. Hopefully, it would be able tell us more later. Above us, the sky turned from deep indigo to almost black. The streetlights had already switched themselves on. The sun took all the heat with it.

But I didn't think that was the only reason I felt cold.

16

"Tetris?" I leaned against his counter, a sack of Angie's muffins in front of me, and two refillable mugs, one filled with tea, one coffee. My ankle was still tender but getting better rapidly enough that I hoped to ditch the crutches soon.

"Be right with you," he called out from the back room. He'd let me in, then scurried to the stock and packing area to get something.

When he emerged, Board Wax trotted happily at his heels, golden fan of a tail wagging. Tetris did not look nearly so happy and carried something in his left hand as if it was something noxious.

"What is it?" I asked.

Once he got closer, he held it out. A small plastic bag with a sealed top, like the kind you'd put a set of earrings in. It was filled with shimmering, iridescent powder that turned from white to pale lavenders, blues, greens, and pinks. The stuff looked as if it was alive and wanted out of the plastic wrapping.

"Faery dust?" I asked.

"What else could it be?"

He set the small bag on the counter. I gestured toward the mug on the right.

"That one's the coffee."

Tetris grabbed the mug as if he were drowning and it was a life raft. Maybe for him it was.

"Where did you get it?" I asked, after we'd both taken a few fortifying sips.

"It was the weirdest thing," he said. "I took Board Wax here out for a run on the beach, and when I passed the area where the main kite guy sets up, Board Wax started whining and scratching. Didn't you boy?"

Board Wax thumped his tail on the floor.

"I pulled him off, not wanting him to eat a rotting bird or get stung by a jellyfish, and that's what I thought this was at first. You know, one of those tiny clear jelly sacks that wash up with the tide?"

As a beach runner, I knew them well. Before Stefon got me some foot sleeves to run in, I used to actually run barefoot. Dodging the tiny jellies was good cardio.

"There was just the one?"

He nodded. "I didn't know what it was, but it looked like drugs and I didn't want some kids stumbling across it while they were building sandcastles, you know?"

His brow furrowed. I shoved the white bakery bag his way. "Have a muffin. Looks like you can use one."

We both munched happily for a while, sipping coffee and tea, not talking. That was one thing I liked about Tetris. Unlike me, he didn't need to talk all the time. Sometimes I even needed a break from myself, you know?

"How well do you know the kite guy?" I finally asked. All the local merchants around Main had some contact with each other, but the beach vendors? They were a different story. Sometimes they talked to us, sometimes they kept to themselves.

Tetris chewed and swallowed. "I've talked to him a time or two, nothing major. I don't even know his name."

"Does he live in town?"

He could, and I wouldn't necessarily know it. Every time I passed the kites on the beach, I was running, and as far as I knew, he'd never been in the bookshop.

"Don't think so. I think he's a couple towns south."

That wasn't unusual, and it wasn't far. The coastal towns squashed right next to each other where the highway ran along the ocean cliffs. But what I wondered was, did that put him outside my jurisdiction? I mean, a Justice is a Justice, but I also didn't want to step on anybody's toes.

"Maybe we can find someone in town who knows him," I said, just musing out loud.

"Someone with kids, maybe?"

When Tetris said that, my stomach lurched. "I really don't like the thought that someone who works with kids so often might be selling contraband like this."

I mean, I'm no prude when it comes to drugs. I have a glass of wine or three every week and am certainly addicted to tea. I have friends who use cannabis regularly, but any kind of drugs and kids don't mix.

"We still don't know the effects of faery dust on humans," I said. "And that worries me."

Board Wax whined. Tetris bent to scratch the dog's head.

"What's the next move?" he asked.

"We have to talk with the kite guy. But I don't want to do it while he's got customers around. Do you know what time he arrives?"

Stefon and I usually ran either after work or before breakfast. He wasn't out in the early morning and was going gangbusters by late afternoons in the summer, and long gone during the winter months, if he came out at all.

"I've seen him setting up around nine-thirty," Tetris said.

"So, we need to talk to him then. But what are we going to say? 'Hey Mr. Kite Guy, are you selling faery contraband?'"

Tetris snorted, but his face looked grim. "I think I can come up with something better than that. But I might want your boyfriend as backup."

That was a good plan, especially as I still couldn't get down to the beach.

There was a banging on the door. Board Wax woofed and ran to the front, where Delta and Preston peered through the glass.

Tetris unlocked the door, and dog, witch, and gnome all did a little *get out of my way, but I'm happy to see you* dance.

"Board Wax!" Tetris said. "Let them come in!"

The dog backed off, and Delta stumbled into the shop.

"Delta, what's wrong?"

She looked out of breath, and her gray hair stuck out as if a rooster had clawed it.

"The kite man!" she huffed.

"We were just talking about him," Tetris replied.

"He's in the hospital."

"Hospital!" I yelped. "What happened?"

"Not sure yet," Delta replied, thunking her tote bag onto the counter.

Tetris flinched, checking to make sure nothing had cracked, but luckily there was a cushion in the bottom of the bag, and sure enough, Preston's little purple hat popped back out.

"We just heard people talking about it," little gnome said.

"Dang," I replied, looking at my watch. "Almost every suspect we have doesn't seem to be suspicious anymore, and I have to get to work."

"I don't know about that," Tetris said, scratching the salt-and-pepper stubble on his chin. Why do people scratch their faces when they're thinking? It's such a strange habit.

"Don't know about what? That I need to open the bookshop?" His comment confused me. Maybe I just wasn't tracking too well.

"No, not that. I mean, just because the surfer dude turned up and kite guy is in the hospital. Doesn't mean they aren't part of the faery dust ring, right? And what about the guy from Saturday market?"

"He's got a point there," Preston said.

"I guess you're right," I replied. "I'll call the hospital today, see if I can get any intel."

I turned to Delta. "And then we need to do some more thinking."

"That we do," the older witch said.

Because if we didn't figure this out, the sprites were going to be pissed, as well as literally grounded. And I didn't want that.

And I also didn't want to have to deal with a disappointed hob.

17

I sent Duncan home and was just closing out the register when the bells at the front door clanged. Tracy and Tabitha rushed in, followed by Carol, who closed the door behind her.

"Would you lock that?" I asked. "And flip the sign?"

It was two minutes to closing, might as well get it done now.

Carol joined the teens at the front counter. The two girls looked fit to burst.

"What's happening?" I asked.

Tabitha smacked a small flyer onto the countertop. It was one of those things I used to call club cards back when Cecilia and I actually did things like live in a city big enough to have nightclubs and had the time and energy to go out to them.

I swear sometimes I felt as if I was living the life of an old person. And being in my late twenties? That was a little sad.

I glanced down at the garishly colored, postcard-sized flyer.

Hush Hush, it said in large, swirling letters. *Sweet super secret good times in Strawberry Cove. Bring your friends but leave the cops at home.*

"Where did you get this?" I asked.

"We were walking near the beach," Tracy said. "And some weird looking raver dude handed it to us. Told us to bring our sweet friends."

Both teens shuddered.

"He was creepy," Tabitha said.

"Creepy how?" All my senses went on high alert. "Did he mess with you?"

Carol lifted her hands. "Already asked. They said he didn't."

Of course, Tracy's mother would have been on it. But the whole thing still disturbed me.

I hoisted myself back up on the stool. Though I hadn't put any weight on my foot, my ankle was still telling me enough was enough.

Both girls looked at each other. Tracy nodded at Tabitha to speak.

"Not sure how to describe it. But he's one of those, you know, older guys trying to pretend they're young and cool?"

"Older. Like how old?" I asked. I remembered well that for a teenager, older could mean anything from twenty-five to eighty.

"I don't know," Tabitha shook her dark bob. The edges of her hair were so sharp, I feared for her chin's safety. "Like, forty, maybe?"

"Ouch," Carol said.

"Oh, Mom. You know what she means."

"Not you, Carol," Tabitha agreed. "You actually *are* cool. You don't have to pretend like it. But yeah, he was also kind of skeezy. You know, that whole 'bring your sweet friends' comment."

"Yeah. Creeped us out. But we thought you should know. In case it has anything to do with the faery dust."

"Good work, you two. This is our first solid lead since Carlson came back and the kite guy was sent to the hospital."

"What?" both teens said.

"He was always nice to me," Tracy chimed in. "I mean, when I was a kid. Remember him, Mom?"

Carol nodded. "Do we know what happened to him?"

"I haven't been able to get any information yet."

Which was strange. Usually, the Seashell Cove gossip line ran on overdrive. But it ran a little slower in summer, just because everyone was too busy to be nosy.

"Delta and Preston told me, but they didn't know any more than what I said."

"So, what do we do now?" Tabitha asked.

I thought a moment.

"Well, are you two willing to go undercover at this thing?"

"That'd be cool!" Tracy said, looking at Tabitha. "Right?"

"I always wanted to be a spy."

Carol sighed. "I'm not too happy about this, but it does make sense. They're the only ones that won't look suspicious at a party like this. But we'll plan it all out, right? And have solid backup?"

Her mouth said yes, but her face and tense shoulders told me she was worried as heck.

I nodded. "I'll get Stefon and Rolf on it. They can be backup, and probably have some elaborately geeky communications devices they're dying to try out."

And Strawberry Cove had a decent overlook and a gently sloping pathway that I might even be able to navigate.

"There's a cave there. That's the likely spot for the party," Tracy said.

It was perfect, actually. Easily accessible but hidden from casual passersby.

"Okay," Carol said, exhaling loudly. "You're sure about Stefon and Rolf? Because cell phone coverage is spotty on the beach."

"Oh, they'll definitely have walkie talkies or something more high tech. I guarantee it."

That's what came from knowing geeks. You had access to geeky tools. "Meanwhile, I have a Wag a Lot meeting to get to. And then we should probably go grill Carlson. And the other thing we need to do?"

"What's that?" Tabitha asked.

"Track down that grig."

"Oh! You know who I bet would know about a grig?" Tracy said, bouncing in her high-top sneakers, face pink with excitement.

"Who?" I racked my brain and came up with nothing.

"Remember that weird alternate universe you and Rhiannon ended up in?"

Rhiannon leapt onto the the counter, startling me. I hadn't even heard her coming. She proceeded to wash her left front paw.

"Yeah, what about it?"

::Think, you dolt,:: Rhiannon said loudly in my head.

Realization dawned. "Oh! You mean Uli the tree spirit?"

"Yeah," Tracy said. "You said Uli seemed wise, right?"

Both teens looked at me expectantly, as Rhiannon pawed at my arm.

::I think we should go.::

"But my meeting!" I looked at my watch.

"Text and tell them you can't come," Carol said.

::She's right. Text them. How hard is handing out dog treats, anyway?::

Hmph. She was right, but that didn't mean I liked it. When did the cat get so savvy about human technology and meetings and all of that?

Rhiannon sneezed and shook her head. *::You think I don't pay attention to everything that goes on in the store, but I do. You humans are always doing something with your phones.::*

"What's she saying?" Tabitha asked.

I looked at the Goth teen. "How do you know she's saying anything?"

Tabitha rolled her eyes at me. "I may not be a hereditary witch, but I'm not stupid."

"She agrees with Carol and says we should visit Uli in his realm."

"In other words," Tabitha started.

"We were right," Tracy finished. The teens high-fived and Carol smiled.

"Carol, you really think this is a good idea?"

"I do. And now is as good a time as any. Especially since I'm here to monitor things. And the teens can go for help if need be."

"You think I'm going to need help?"

All of them turned and just stared at me silently. Including Rhiannon. I bristled. Uli was great, but that realm was kind of creepy.

"Why are you all ganging up on me?"

"Sarah," Carol's voice was gentle, as if she was about to explain something to a small child and didn't want to upset it. "You're known for getting yourself into sticky situations."

"And you've been a little accident-prone lately," Tabitha said.

I straightened my spine.

"I'll have you know that I'm a witch and a Justice."

They all smiled.

"We know," Carol said. "And that's why we're going to let you do it. Otherwise, we'd all sit on you and make you stay at home."

"Fine," I huffed. "You remember which book was the portal?"

"On it!" Tabitha replied, and the teens scurried to the back of the store.

Carol leaned across the counter, face intent. "You're the only one who can do this, Sarah."

"What do you mean? Isn't it something any witch can do?"

"It doesn't appear so. You know how you're always jealous of the way your Uncle Cyrus can pop in and out of space and time?"

"Yeah." As a matter of fact, he was probably in Paris right now. Again. Just when I needed him.

"Well, I think you can do that with alternate magical dimensions."

"Really? Hmm. I never thought of it that way."

"I'm just saying..." Carol wiggled her fingers as if making a magical gesture.

::*Yeah, just saying,*:: Rhiannon echoed.

When four people I trusted told me something, I

needed to listen. I guess this was another wake-up call for Sarah Endora Braxton.

"All right. Let's head to the back. And could you grab an ottoman for me?"

If I was traveling into an alternate dimension, I needed to be comfortable.

We headed to Biff's Corner. I flopped into the comfy reading chair set in the back corner as Rhiannon perched on the shelf where the gargoyle had been. The teens leaned against a couple of bookcases.

Once I got settled, I looked at Tracy's mom. Blond and slender, in neat jeans and summer sandals, she looked nothing like an accountant. Or a witch. Carol stood in the center of the aisle, body loose, face perfectly calm. But then, she wasn't the one about to fall through a book and into a truly weird space.

"Are you all right?" she asked.

"I guess so. It's just weird thinking of doing this of my own volition. I'm used to getting yanked here and there, so I'm not sure exactly the best protocol to go about this."

"Well," she said, "what happened last time?"

"I was reading that book—" I pointed, and Tabitha waved it in the air in illustration "—and just kind of tumbled in."

"Okay. Well, this time," Carol said, "try going through your usual magical protocols. You know, centering and all that. Turn to the page you remember and will yourself there."

::Wait!:: Rhiannon thought very loudly in my head. *::You need to set up a protocol to get out, too. Remember?::*

"Right. Thanks, cat."

"What'd she say?" Tracy asked.

"She reminded me that I need to set up a way to get us out of there. So we don't get flung out, like last time."

::*Set up a way to get* you *out. I know my way around just fine, thank you.*::

I smiled.

"Well, that insulted her," I said out loud. "Correction. I need a way to get myself out. Rhiannon said she can take care of herself."

"That's good," Carol said. "Because I have no idea how we'd get a cat to do anything."

I swear Rhiannon smirked.

18

"All right," I said. "Let's do this."

Tabitha handed me the book. *Unexplained Mysteries of the Faery Kind* was written in gilt lettering on the embossed leather cover. I flipped through the pages the way you'd do through Tarot cards: half looking and half feeling, trying to sense the page that drew me in before.

When I reached it, somewhere around one third into the book, I felt a sort of magical snap.

"That's it," I said.

Book open on my lap, feet propped up on the ottoman, I focused on the breath moving in and out of my lungs.

Rhiannon leapt up onto the arm of the chair and sat, alert and ready. I closed my eyes, slowed my breathing down, and found the deep anchor that rested in my center, in that place between the solar plexus and the pelvis.

I slowly traced a clockwise spiral onto the page,

reciting a magical cantrip out loud. This would be our entry and exit door.

"When I open my eyes and read out loud, to the realm I shall travel with ease. And once in the realm, when ready to leave, I shall ride home as light as a breeze."

I opened my eyes again looked at my friends and shared a green-eyed gaze with Rhiannon for a moment.

"All right, here goes," I said. I traced the spiral on the page as I read the words and then, just as before, I was tumbling, falling, flying.

But this time, it felt gentler, and I landed softly in the other realm instead of crash landing.

I was greeted by the sound of the Babbling Brook. "Merry, Humphrey, Faery, Foo. Wizards laughing. Primal goo."

Rhiannon landed gracefully at my side.

We both looked around. The place was just as magical as before. The Babbling Brook was still a multicolored flow of water—like the marbled end papers of a rare book —splashing over rocks. Golden sun shone through pink and purple clouds, just as it had before, and silver and bronze birds chirped from ochre trees that were neither apple, nor cherry, nor maple, but some strange version of all three.

It was breathtaking, really. So oddly colored and uncanny, the way magic places often are.

"Is that the witch Umserrah?"

The rustling, papery voice was Uli, the tree person. I looked around and sure enough, moving slowly toward me was the great majestic ent, with a large trunk and waving branches. Knotholes formed kindly eyes and a mouth.

He called me Umserrah because I was so flustered when we first met, I could barely recall my own name.

"Uli." I bowed my head. "Pardon us for intruding on your realm, again. But we have need of your help."

"You are always welcome here, Umserrah the witch, and you as well, Rhiannon the cat. What assistance do you require?"

The ent came to a stop next to us and I could feel it rooting in the earth, which was a very strange thing indeed. The large tree looked at me and frowned.

"But first, are you injured, witch Umserrah?"

I shrugged. "Twisted my ankle. It's nothing major."

The ent *tsk tssked* at me. "Nothing major is the perfect sort of injury!"

"What?"

"The Babbling Brook specializes in curing minor wounds."

Minor wounds? This was some serious D&D territory.

I looked at the Babbling Brook. It was laughing and splashing. "Primal goo. Faery foo. Humpback. Flowers. Sherrie Lou!"

"Seriously?"

"Yes. Dangle your feet in the waters as we speak."

Rhiannon's shoulders shook with laughter. I scowled but hobbled my way to the creek bed and flopped down. I took off my sneakers and rolled up my jeans, then gazed into the multicolored water and sniffed. It smelled okay. Pretty good, actually. Like cherry soda.

I gingerly placed one foot, then the other, into the water. It swirled and laughed around me, tickling my toes.

"No tickling!" I admonished. "And can you sing more quietly, please?" The water stopped with the tickling, thank the Goddess, and lowered its voice to a gurgle.

That was better. Now maybe I could have an actual conversation.

"The water feels pretty good, Rhiannon. You should try it."

She hissed, eyes wide with horror. I laughed, then looked up at Uli, who had moved closer to the water. Time to get what we came for.

"We need to know what knowledge you have of grigs."

"Ah, grigs," Uli replied. "Grigs are charming creatures."

"No, they are not," a second voice said with a snort.

I looked up. Across the Babbling Brook was Serafina the black centaur. She was beautiful and more than a little intimidating.

"Grigs are obnoxious little troublemakers." The black centaur tossed her human head as if she had a mane, which she most assuredly did not.

"Now Serafina," Uli sighed, "you are too harsh. Grigs all mean well."

"Meaning well and acting well are two different things entirely. I will have no part of this foolish conversation."

The centaur looked at me and snapped her teeth. "But you, witch, you keep Seashell Cove safe, do you hear me? I do not like the goings-on of late."

Well, that made two of us.

The centaur turned to go.

"Wait, please, Serafina," I said. "What do you know about the stolen faery dust?"

She stopped, working her mouth as if chewing on a particularly sour apple.

"All I know is that bad creatures are doing bad things, and if you do not fix this, the sprites are in danger of extermination."

::*And?*:: Rhiannon interjected.

"And, friend cat, should the sprites be exterminated, all of us are in trouble," Serafina replied.

"The centaur is correct," said Uli. "You cannot take one small thing from the realm and expect the whole to remain healthy and sound."

"Find whoever did this, witch Sarah." Serafina's amber eyes flashed with worry and anger.

"I'll do my best. But if you or the other centaurs have information, that will be useful."

"I shall inquire."

She trotted off through the strange forest, black coat dappled with the strange sun.

"She's always busy, that one," said Uli. "But now, grigs. Grigs are carefree and cheerful and simply want everyone to have a good time."

"And," I said, "this time?"

"Sometimes what grigs consider to be fun and jolly is not so fun or jolly for those they have roped into their shenanigans."

"Great," I said. "It sounds like a party with dangerous drunk."

"Oh yes," Uli said, nodding his tree had gravely. "That is their specialty. Grigs enjoy the intoxication of others and feed off it and can make their mischief far and wide, heedless of the harm."

I could tell it pained the ent to admit to such a thing. I got the feeling that Uli only wished to speak well of others.

"Why does no one stop them?" I asked.

Uli looked across the Babbling Brook, who was still singing quietly away.

"It is hard to. One often thinks that the grigs have

learned their lesson and will act this way no more. But their nature overtakes them. And as I said, they do not see the harm in it."

::*Well, we shall make them see the harm,*:: Rhiannon said.

I looked at the little black cat, my grumpy accomplice in whatever the heck this situation was.

"At least we know where to find this particular grig."

Uli looked interested.

"How do you plan to do that, witch Umserrah?"

"There's a big party in a few days' time, and I have a feeling they're behind it."

"Yes, that is wise. Go where there is frivolity and the grig is surely not far away."

"But you're there's no way to find them beforehand? To stop this thing before it starts?"

The ent shook his branches.

"I do not see a way. But if I do hear anything, I shall send word."

"All right, Uli. Thank you."

I took one last look around the strange realm, wishing I could spend more time there exploring the pathways through the woods. The trees blinked at me. One grinned, showing stubby wooden teeth.

That was weird. Why would a tree need teeth?

"Friend Uli," I said, "might I bring more visitors some other time?"

The teens would seriously love this place. Stefon, too, come to think of it. It was straight out of one of his fantasy novels.

"You and your friends are always welcome here. I have many things to show you, should you wish to see them, and many things to teach you should you wish to learn."

Wow. That was a large offer. And I knew it. I had a

feeling ents did not offer to teach very many who were not of their kind.

With a slight bow of my head, I said, "I give thanks to you, friend Uli. I shall return. Ready Rhiannon?"

::Ready.::

I took a deep breath, breathing in the tangy sense of forest loam, apple blossoms and honey, and cherry soda.

I listened to the babbling of the brook and found my own center.

Then I grabbed my shoes in my left hand and raised my right. Tracing a spiral in the air, I spoke out loud.

"We wish to return home now, swiftly and with ease. We wish to return home now. Help us magic, please."

And with a wish and a thump, I was back in the armchair, Rhiannon perched at my side.

Both teens gasped, and Carol smiled.

"That was so cool!" Tabitha said.

"Can you teach me?" Tracy replied.

I blinked my eyes and stretched.

"I can try. But right now, I need a cup of tea."

19

I might not have been ready to run yet, but I really needed to get out and be by the ocean. My ankle really was feeling better. The Babbling Brook's powers must be formidable. I wasn't yet ready to tackle the steep steps down to our main beach, or to run a 10K, but I was well enough to at least test out my ankle on the soft sand of the beaches of Strawberry Cove.

Stefon kindly picked me up from the shop and drove me out to do some reconnaissance. We both wanted to see where the party might be.

"Sure you're good to walk, babe?"

"I think so."

"Well, I'm going to carry your crutches all the same."

I had to admit that was a good idea. I would hate to get halfway across the sand and have my boyfriend need to carry me back to the car.

Just off the small parking lot was a pathway through some scrub pine trees and sandy soil dotted with wild strawberries. Stefon had my crutches in one hand and my arm linked into his other.

"Good?" he asked.

"Good."

And it was. I was walking gingerly and in no hurry and had put my barefoot running shoes on for a little added traction. It felt nice to walk on the mix of sand and soil.

The pathway opened after a small rise, and I paused to take in a deep breath as the expanse of sand and ocean spread out in front of us.

"Dang, that's pretty," I said.

"It is," Stefon replied. "That's why I live here."

I poked his ribs. "I thought that was me."

"Babe. I moved here long before I met you. I *stay* half because of you, half for this ocean. Otherwise, I'd live in a place where there are a lot more Black people. Trust me."

"Point taken," I said. We continued walking on the soft sand. The Strawberry Cove beach was much less wild than the one at Seashell Cove, and, of course, there were no sheer drop cliffs here to navigate. Which I appreciated.

"This is all right," I said. "I might actually be able to do the one-K."

"Let's not get ahead of ourselves, Sarah. Now, where do you think this party's gonna be?"

Drat. He was right, but I really did miss running.

"Well, the teens seem to think there's a cave around here, but I've never seen it. I don't come to this beach very often."

And hadn't since I was a small child. The memory of my mother and father, laughing as I got drenched in the shallows, gave me a pang. Good memories, but ones that brought back their loss too keenly.

"Hmm..." I said as I caught sight of the flap of brightly colored kites overhead. There was a rainbow box kite, a green dragon, and a blue fish, as well as some yellow and orange classic diamond shapes.

"I didn't realize they had kites at this beach."

"Me either," Stefon replied.

"I wonder if they know the kite guy from Seashell Cove."

Stefon looked down at me. "Sure you want to ask?"

I shrugged. "We still don't have the information we need. There's no guarantee this party is going to actually happen or that a grig or faery dust will be there. And something happened with the kite guy, and no hospital on earth will give out personal information."

"All right. Let's go."

We made our way carefully across the sand, dodging some rocks, shells, and a few tiny jellyfish blobs. This beach didn't get the big, downed trees like ours did. Made me wonder why.

As we approached the kite seller, she looked up, surprised, almost as if she was expecting us but was afraid we were going to show up. Okay, that was weird.

I gave a small wave.

"Hi there," I said when we got close enough to not shout. "I didn't know anyone sold kites out here. We're used to them at Seashell Cove, though. That's where we're from."

She looked at me warily, her dark hair crisscrossing her face as a breeze lifted it.

Luckily, I'd firmly anchored my own thick hair before we left the car.

She raked a hand through her hair and secured the errant strands with a rubber band.

"Been out here just the summer," she said, shading her eyes with one hand. "Trying it out."

"Get much business?" Stefon asked.

The woman shrugged. "I do okay. Not sure if I'll be back next summer or not."

"So," Stefon said, "We've heard there are a lot of parties out this way."

"Do you ever see that? The parties?" I asked.

"I'm gone before then. I sell to families with kids, not teenagers and college students who want to get hopped up on who knows what."

"Drugs?" Stefon asked.

She shrugged again. "Can't say."

Can't say, or won't say? I thought.

"So, do you know the Seashell Cove kite guy?" Stefon asked.

Her eyes widened, then her face shut down.

"We met a time or two," she said, "when I was starting out. But I can't say I knew him."

"Well. You heard he was in the hospital, right?" I said. "And do you know his name?"

"I did hear that. I think his name is Stuart."

Stuart. I turned to Stefon.

"That's the name of the guy from the Saturday Craft Fair. The one Carlson mentioned."

A family approached with two shrieking children in tow.

"Look, I don't know what you're looking for, or why you came here to ask me questions, but I have to work now. Leave me in peace."

"All right. But if you know anything…" I began.

"I don't," she said, voice and eyes flat.

Then she turned, plastering on a huge smile and waving at the children who ran her way.

"Let's keep going, babe. You want to still find the cave or go back to the car?"

I put a little more weight onto my ankle. It seemed to be holding.

"Let's see if we can find the cave."

I was enjoying being outside in the evening sun and wasn't quite ready to go home yet. We walked farther, past a few more families enjoying the sunny evening, though most were packing up. They had to get the kiddos fed. My own stomach growled, reminding me it was getting on towards dinner.

"What's that?" Stefon pointed. I looked towards the shallow dunes in the trees. And sure enough, there was a dark spot.

"Looks like a hollow of some sort."

"Or a cave?" Stefon asked.

Or a cave.

We headed that direction. A man jogged past, saw us, slowed, and circled back.

"Hey. You two like to have fun?"

Something about him gave me the creeps.

"Sure," Stefon said, putting on a strange, jocular attitude. I looked at him as if I'd never seen him before, but then quickly recovered.

"Sure," I echoed.

The guy handed us one of the club cards.

"In a couple days, it's gonna be wild around here. Tell your friends."

"Will do."

He set off again, but I called after his retreating back.

"Hey, wait!" I flipped over the flyer. The back side was blank, just like the one the teens had. "Do you know who is the event planner for this? I might be looking for someone to help me with promotions."

"Oh yeah. Yeah, he's a good guy, but prefers not to give out his name. You know how it is. He's not exactly getting park permits to rent the cave."

Right.

"How can we get a hold of him?" Stefon asked.

"Magic Fairy Dust dot com, dude." Then he raced off. "Gotta run."

"Magic Fairy Dust dot com? You have got to be kidding me."

Sometimes the clues were so obvious, they smacked you in the face like a trout.

Now we just needed to figure out if Magic Fairy Dust dot Com guy, Stuart, and the bad man, were one and the same.

Though if Stuart was the one in the hospital, I couldn't see how the party was still on.

"You think a grig can throw a party on its own?" I asked.

"Guess we're going to find out."

20

"The council is unhappy," Uncle Cyrus said, taking a sip of his ruby-red wine, silver rings flashing in the sun that streamed through the giant plate glass windows. As usual, it was the most expensive Cabernet Sauvignon on Costas' menu. I was never exactly clear where my dandy warlock of an uncle got his money.

I sipped my own Pinot Grigio, trying to concentrate on what Cyrus was saying, which was difficult given the view of the ocean outside.

I swear, I've lived in Seashell Cove almost my whole life, but that view never gets old.

"When is the council ever happy?" I retorted.

Cyrus raised an eyebrow and cut into his steak. I forked up a mouthful of my mushroom risotto, which was covered in yummy freshly grated Parmesan cheese. Next to me, Stefon silently ate his sea bass and drank his local beer, some sort of pale lager. He always said he wasn't picky about what type of beer it was, as long as it was good.

"What's the council concerned about now?" I asked after swallowing.

"Grigs." Cyrus set his knife and fork down, picked up his wineglass and swirled the contents in a dizzying spiral of reds and purples. "They are very concerned that the grigs are causing mischief again. And they're worried that people are going to get hurt this time."

"Mischief again?" Stefon asked.

This was news to me, too.

"Yes. We've tried to keep it quiet, but there have been incidents in multiple places."

"What exactly happens?" I said, then stuffed another forkful of creamy mushroomy goodness into my mouth.

"They're concerned, for one, that grigs are trafficking in contraband faery dust, which you already know."

"What I don't understand," Stefon said, "and you know, maybe this is a thing that you're not supposed to say to humans, but, what exactly is the danger with faery dust?"

"Sarah?" Uncle Cyrus asked.

Great. He was testing me. Testing my knowledge as if I were a teenager again.

I took another sip of crisp wine, stalling for time as I racked my brain. Faery dust. Faery dust. Faery dust. What did I know?

"Well, the smaller fae, like sprites, use it to fuel some of their magic and it helps them fly. Kind of like the dust on a butterfly's wings."

"And what happens if they run out?"

I shook my head. "I'm not one hundred percent sure, but since it gives them longevity and their magic shine, it can't be good."

"Okay," Stefon sipped his beer, looking thoughtful. "I get the part that it's detrimental to the sprites, but how would someone other than sprites use it? Like, other faeries or something."

"It can be used as a mild intoxicant," Uncle Cyrus said.

I remembered the rest then.

"Right! It's not too severe, but it gives you a lift and makes parties more fun."

"Got it in one," Cyrus replied, then attacked the mound of grilled vegetables on his plate.

"But how about humans?" Stefon asked again.

Well, and wasn't that the million-dollar question?

"Is it a toxin, Uncle Cyrus?" I had to admit defeat. This I didn't remember. At all.

"It's in the protocols," he said. "You have the information somewhere in the worksheets."

"Yes. Yes." I waved my hands. "I should know all this. I know. But I don't, so can you just tell us please?"

On the other hand, he was right. I should have looked this up as soon as I first heard about it. Not that I would admit that out loud.

"It can cause a euphoria so great in humans that their hearts stop beating."

"Wow," Stefon said, setting down his beer glass with a thunk. "Do they at least die happy?"

"They do, at that," Uncle Cyrus said.

"But they still die," I said. "So, this party is more dangerous than we thought before."

"It is," Cyrus continued, "which is why the council is so concerned. There have been several unexplained deaths that have happened at parties. In Paris. Singapore. Mexico City. Edinburgh..."

"That means we have to stop the party, right?" Stefon said.

I slid my hand into his.

"No," I said, as Uncle Cyrus shook his head. "It means we have to go ahead as planned. We need to check out the guy's website and find a way to infiltrate and stop whoever's doing this. Then catch the grig, find the stolen faery dust, and put an end to the trafficking operation."

And putting an end to a trafficking operation is a lot more work than stopping a party.

My heart sank.

"The council is on it," Uncle Cyrus said. "I told them about your plans, and Ah Lam Wu will be meeting me here to discuss our options."

"You're calling in agents? Like secret spies? Is that what your girlfriend is? Part of the super-secret witches and warlocks spy branch of the council?"

Cyrus grimaced. "We are not teenagers and therefore she is not my girlfriend."

But I noticed he didn't say whether she was a spy. I knew what that meant. She definitely was.

"Do I need to be briefed or something?"

"It's on a need-to-know basis. But Sarah, you're in charge of your friends and you're the one who must make certain they remain safe."

His eyes were grave.

I picked up my water glass and gulped, suddenly flushed with anxiety. I mean, I knew I was Justice, but sometimes I wished I wasn't.

"Can't you do that last part?"

But I saw the answer in my uncle's eyes. And I *knew* the answer even before I spoke the words.

Stefon reached out and squeezed my hand. "It's all right, babe. You have a posse."

I smiled at him, because yeah, I did. But my smile was still tinged with worry that gnawed at my heart.

I really hoped no one was going to get hurt.

21

I was struggling. Fighting. Lashing out at a shadowy being who dodged and feinted, swooped and menaced. Where was my magic? I needed it. Now.

But the glowing core at my center that I was so used to tapping in to—easily as breathing—was absent. My magic was gone. Stolen.

I could no longer fly.

The figure closed in. A large hand enveloped me.

I was trapped.

"Sarah! Sarah! Wake up!"

Stefon's voice brought me back.

"Whaaa?" I looked around in confusion, taking in the details of the electric fireplace, flames glowing blue and green today, the television above it. The floor-length curtains, covering the large windows that, during the day, looked out over the ocean.

And Stefon, his warm, dark eyes staring at me in concern, his gaming headphones worn like a scarf around his neck.

"You were dreaming."

He stroked a hand down my thigh, his warmth reaching my skin beneath my jeans. The book I'd been reading was splayed on the big sofa next to me, and the tea in the mug on the coffee table no longer had steam rising from its surface.

"How long was I asleep?"

He sat next to me, drawing me into the circle of his arms.

"Not sure. I was still working on this new design, listening to music, when I heard you thrashing around."

We'd gone back to his apartment after dinner. I had needed to talk through some of our conversation over dinner. We needed a new plan before meeting up with Carol, Delta, Toby, Cecilia, and the teens. I also knew Rhiannon would have plenty to say about the case and I didn't want to hear it without that plan.

After we talked awhile, Stefon had gone to finish one piece of his current project and I'd curled up on the sofa to read. For some reason, I hadn't wanted to be alone.

"What was the dream?" he asked, stroking my hair and pulling me into his solid chest.

"I think I was a sprite. All I know is I was in danger."

"What kind of danger?"

"It was a person, but I couldn't see them. And I'm not sure if they were human, or a witch, or something else, but they were threatening me. When you woke me up, they had just grabbed me. I fit in their hand."

Stefon kissed my temple as I stared into the flames. The flickering blue tongues reminded me of the sprites in Toby's garden. Lively. Beautiful. Dangerous if crossed.

"Want some more tea? Something else?"

"A kiss?"

"That I can do, my lady."

He pressed his warm lips against mine, slowly at first, his soft, curly beard tickling my face. I deepened the kiss, clutching at his T-shirt with my hands, then broke away.

"Thanks," I whispered, looking into those bottomless eyes.

"Anytime, babe."

We sat back on the couch, still touching. I sighed.

"You gonna call Cecilia?"

"I guess I should. See if Toby has any insight."

But I didn't want to. I didn't want any of this.

"Are we putting the teenagers in danger?"

I felt him shrug. "Possibly. But a bunch of us will be there to make sure they stay safe. Rolf even offered to show up, and you know Tetris and Angie will do anything to protect this town. And to help you."

Something inside me relaxed at his words. I felt the truth of them. I had friends. Family, even. As usual, I started out thinking I needed to figure out all the answers, but the answer was always to trust the people around me. We were a team now. A strange and wacky team, to be sure, but a team nonetheless.

"Stefon, when you're Dungeon Master, how do you make sure everyone works together? What's the key?"

He stroked his beard. "You turning into a geek, babe?" I heard the smile in his voice.

"Not likely. I'll remain a nerd, thank you very much."

The distinction between nerd and geek was a discussion we returned to often, and a source of amusement for our friends.

Until they got sick of it and shut us down.

"Well, a good Dungeon Master not only sets up the perimeters of the adventure, but they also make sure that the people taking part have a variety of skills and talents."

"So, everyone plays a part."

"Not only that. Everyone's part is integral to the whole campaign. If one person dies, the stakes change."

"And the stakes are?"

He shifted on the sofa so he could look at me.

"The stakes are always different, but they always have to do with facing or warding off danger, disaster, or death."

"The Three Ds?"

He laughed. "I guess you could call them that. And this is just my experience, both as a player and as DM. Other gamers might tell you different."

As I was pondering that, a knock came at the door.

Stefon's head whipped toward the apartment entry. "What the heck?"

He padded off to see who was there. My senses went on high alert, and I rose from the sofa, thankful that my ankle was holding weight again. I really needed to thank Uli and the Babbling Brook for whatever healing magic they'd worked on me. It was nice to be free of the pain.

Free of the pain. Something about that phrase rang in my head, telling me it was important.

Stefon returned with Cecilia and Toby, the hob looking a bit green at being so far away from their garden and home.

"What are you two doing here?"

"Why don't you answer your phone! I've been texting and calling for an hour!" Cecilia said. "I finally decided to track you down. You weren't at the store, so I came here."

I looked down at the small black brick of my phone on

Stefon's coffee table. "Sorry. I fell asleep while reading and didn't check."

My fuchsia-haired friend stomped across the space, as much as a short Asian woman in socks could, and glared at me.

But behind the glare, I sensed her fear.

I looked back at Toby, but the hob was studiously avoiding my gaze, eyes trained on the dancing flames.

"Can I get anyone tea? Water? Soda? Alcoholic beverages?" Stefon asked.

No one answered.

I flopped back down on the couch. "If you're just going to stand there and glare at me, I'm getting off my ankle."

It was a lot better since my visit to Uli's realm, but I still needed to baby it a bit.

"Oh! I'm so sorry!" Cecilia said, sitting down beside me and taking one of my hands in hers. "I'm just so worried."

I looked from her, to Stefon, to Toby, whom Stefon was gently trying to get farther into the living room space so they could sit down.

Toby was weeping. Long, slow tears etched silvery tracks down their golden-brown skin.

"Toby?" Cecilia's voice was light as a butterfly. "Can you sit down and tell Sarah and Stefon what happened?"

The hob nodded. I scooched over on the sofa to make more room. Cecilia moved with me, leaving space for Toby's thin frame on the end of the gray sofa. Stefon bustled around in the tiny kitchen for a minute, returning with four glasses of water, which he set on the coffee table before sitting in the armchair nearest the fire. Good thing the thing was in summer mode, and not giving off any heat.

I love my cottage's wood burner, but it's nice to have a fire year 'round.

Toby took a long drink, swiped at their face, blew their nose in a voluminous green handkerchief, and finally looked around, blinking, as if they had been elsewhere.

"The sprites…"

Toby took in a long, shuddering breath. Cecilia patted their back in encouragement.

"Tell them, Toby. They can help."

"The sprites are getting weaker. A lot weaker. And they said if you aren't going to do anything to help them, they'll do it themselves."

"What?" I asked, gobsmacked. "Why don't they think I'm doing anything? I've done nothing but work on this case."

Well, that and run my bookshop during busy season, and nurse my injured ankle, and fall asleep on my boyfriend's couch. But a witch needs a break sometimes, right?

"More faery dust is missing, they got word of some big party, and they're really mad."

"Okay." We didn't know about the more faery dust part, but the party? "We're already on the party. That's our big plan. We're sending the teens in to infiltrate so we can catch whoever it is."

"They want you to stop it."

"Stop the party." Stefon's words were more a statement than a question, which was usually his way of saying, are you sure about that?

"I told them it wasn't possible," Cecilia interjected, then shrugged helplessly.

Because sprites weren't the most reasonable creatures when they felt threatened.

The dream came back to me now, full force. In the dream, I couldn't find my magic.

And that's what the sprites must be going through.

"Toby?" I asked. "How much magic do the sprites have left?"

22

Turns out the sprites were so frantic because their magic was depleting at a seriously rapid rate.

I called an emergency meeting for before the shop opened, and got on the horn with Uncle Cyrus, making sure that the council would make good on their offer of help. Because otherwise, what good were they if they couldn't protect magical beings? Especially the smaller ones who were very important to all the ecosystems but were easily overlooked in favor of their larger, stronger counterparts.

Cyrus promised me that he and his maybe, maybe-not girlfriend, Ms. Wu, had some magical tech figured out and would meet us at Toby and Cecilia's in the morning. So here we were, standing around the small garden on a pleasant summer morning, smelling the herbs and flowers.

Well, I was sitting, sipping tea, and Tetris leaned on the rail of the deck next to my boyfriend, nursing a go cup of coffee. My ankle was much better, but it still needed more rest than usual. Being a hob, Toby couldn't help themselves, so of course, there were two different kinds of tea available as we waited for the teenagers, Carol, Delta, and Preston.

Even Rhiannon had insisted on coming, which was unusual. The only two places she usually liked to be were, first and foremost, the store, and during the winter months, my house. And that was mostly because the house had a fireplace, not because she wanted to spend any extra time with me. She was stalking through the garden somewhere. I just hoped she wasn't intent on killing anything and was glad Board Wax wasn't in attendance. Tetris had left the dog at the shop. Which reminded me, I should text Liam and make sure the innkeeper was keeping an eye on the wastrel, Carlson.

The sprites, whom I had last seen buzzing around like hummingbirds or bees, looked forlorn and had lost some of their natural shine. Four of them huddled beneath a lavender bush, heads hanging.

"That's worrisome," I said to Cecilia. "They really do look sick."

Toby looked mournful and fluttered their hands in helplessness and distress.

"I know, Toby. I'm sorry. But Uncle Cyrus said he's bringing something to help."

I hoped that whatever he and Ms. Wu had cooked up turned out to be actually helpful, because it was clear the sprites were desperate. I took another sip of English Breakfast tea and scanned the garden, hoping a solution to all our problems would materialize inside my head. As if.

Finally, there was a rattling of the gate. And in walked Cyrus and Ah Lam Wu. They were followed by Delta Crabbit, looking windswept and grumpy. Both warlocks were sharply dressed as always, both wearing dark linen trousers and lightweight linen shirts. Cyrus's shirt was pale lavender and Ms. Wu's was stark white. The bald dome of Cyrus's head looked polished to a dark sheen and Ah Lam Wu had an impressive fall of straight, dark hair. The two of them really belonged in Paris or Singapore or San Francisco. Not Portland. And certainly not Seashell Cove.

I set down my mug and rose. Uncle Cyrus carried what looked like a plain wooden box in his arms.

"What is that thing?" Tetris asked.

"What does it look like?" Delta Crabbit said. "It's a box. And considering who's carrying it, probably a magical one."

Tetris nodded and slurped at his reusable coffee go cup.

"Give me a moment, please," Cyrus said. "Let me set this on the table and I'll explain."

"Toby," Ms. Wu said, "can you bring the sprites over?"

Toby nodded and ran over to the herb garden where the sprites were languishing.

Carol and the teens walked into the back yard just then and stopped to watch as the hob held out their skinny arms over the garden bed. The sprites literally crawled onto them, allowing the hob to carry them back to our little seating area on the deck outside the kitchen and place them carefully on the table.

Carol, Tabitha, and Tracy followed, leaning against the deck railing near Tetris. Rhiannon leapt up on the railing, too, as the teens scratched her head in tribute.

Uncle Cyrus sat next to me at the table and looked at the sprites, face serious. Ah Lam pulled up a chair as well and began fiddling with some clasps on the box.

"Sprites," Uncle Cyrus said, "the council is saddened to hear of your misfortune and want you to know that we are putting our full support behind Sarah and her friends in tracking down who did this to you and stopping anyone else from getting hurt. But in order to do that, we have to allow the party to continue as planned."

The green sprite, Rowena, gave an tiny, angry squawk.

Cyrus held up a hand. "I know. I know you want the party stopped, but in order to actually stop the harm being done, we need to catch the people doing it. If we stop the party before it begins, they will be alerted and escape."

The sprites looked at me and I nodded in agreement.

Cyrus, Ms. Wu, and I had all discussed this on the call the night before.

"What we have here..." Uncle Cyrus began. He gestured to the box, then looked at Ah Lam to continue. She motioned for him to go on, but Cyrus shook his head.

"The best way to explain it," she said, "is that it acts sort of like a magical Faraday cage."

"A what?" asked Tabitha.

"That is very dope!" Stefon said.

"We are hoping that it will retain the magic you have left and protect you from any further attack," Ms. Wu continued.

"What do you mean, hoping?" Toby said, voice fierce. We looked at the usually quiet hob in shock. "Hoping is not good enough."

The hob crossed their arms over their skinny chest, a mulish look on their face.

"I don't blame you for being concerned, Toby," I said. "But all magic is experimental."

"And how many times have you two tested this?" chimed in Delta. Good question.

"Three times," Ah Lam said, "and the third time, it worked very well."

"And the first two times?" Toby growled.

Cyrus and Ah Lam looked at each other. I could tell they didn't want to speak.

"The first time," Cyrus said gently, "the being still languished and died. The second time, it worked to protect the magical being from outside attack."

"And the third time," Ah Lam said, "both protection and retention of magic worked."

I leaned forward, looking at the sprites.

"I know this isn't perfect, but it's the best we have right now. It's our only option. And with you as weak as you are, I think we should risk it. What do you think?"

The sprites looked at each other, and then back at me, then at the box.

"We'll do it," Rowena said.

Ah Lam and Uncle Cyrus both relaxed. I hadn't realized how tense they were before.

Ah Lam undid a golden clasp at the front of the box and opened the lid.

We all gasped. Inside, the box gleamed like gold. It was beautiful, and sparkled with magic. Oddly enough, it also felt, well, homey. There was something comforting about it, even. As I watched, the four sprites relaxed as well.

"It will do," Rowena said. The green sprite looked too worn out to be pleased. "But now we must rest again. Can we do so in this contraption?"

"Of course," Uncle Cyrus replied. "We wish to help you retain as much of your remaining magic as possible."

Toby held out their arms and the sprites climbed on the hob. Then Toby carefully placed their arms near the box and the sprites slid down. I leaned forward to peer inside of the box and was pleased to find there were flowers and cushions strewn about, a few small air plants on the sides, and what looked like bottles of nectar placed strategically in the corners.

The sprites would be comfortable at least, and hopefully we'd be able to free them within the next twenty-four hours.

Once the sprites were settled, Ah Lam shut the box again and fastened the front clasp and the side latches as well.

"It's sealed now," she said, then she pulled a golden lock from her pocket and secured the main closure. "And now no one can break in."

"Magically, or otherwise," said Cyrus.

"What if someone steals the box?" Tracy asked.

Hmm, that was a good point, and one I hadn't thought of. Leave it to the teenagers to think of it.

"The box stays with me," Uncle Cyrus said.

"With both of us," said Ah Lam.

Both my uncle and his maybe sort-of girlfriend looked fierce and determined.

"I wouldn't cross them," Stefon murmured.

I wouldn't either. And I'm a witch.

"All right! Let's get the rest of this meeting started," I said. "Everyone, pull up a chair, grab some tea, and let's finalize our plan. Because Tetris and I both have shops to open, and you all have things to do."

There was much scuffling and rearranging of chairs with Toby and Cecilia running back and forth, refreshing the tea and grabbing more mugs.

Just as we settled in, Angie came waltzing in the back, followed by Buster. Both of their arms were filled with bags and boxes that smelled tantalizingly of muffins.

Buster looked around curiously, his eyebrows raising when he saw the box.

"That's pretty," he said.

"Thank you," Ms. Wu said.

Why had Angie brought Buster along? Was he here snooping or something? Once this situation was done, I was going to have to sit down for a serious talk with Buster and find out exactly what kind of magic he carried.

I noticed Cyrus also giving him the eye. Good.

"We can't stay," Angie said. "But I wanted to help, and this is all I know how to do." She motioned to Buster, who set his bakery boxes down, not saying a word.

"Angie," I said, hand over my heart, "this is the best ever."

She smiled and waved, motioning for Buster to go ahead, and they traipsed off through the garden gate. I grabbed a fragrant blueberry muffin from the first box and took a bite.

Pure bliss. Then I swallowed and looked around me.

"Let's get down to business. We need protection for the teens, some sort of communication system, and a plan."

23

After work, I sat in my living room with Uncle Cyrus and Ah Lam Wu, the box that held my mother's crystal ball on the coffee table between us.

"Have you heard from Carol or Delta?" Uncle Cyrus asked, sipping at a glass of seltzer water.

I nodded. "Carol said they got some protective amulets made today, so that's good." The amulets would give Tracy and Tabitha some shielding at the party, both from random magic and, hopefully, from the effects of the faery dust. "The teens are checking out the Fairy Dust website, and Stefon and Rolf figured out some sort of coms system."

Cell phone coverage on the beaches was spotty, so handing that chore off to our local tech geeks was a relief.

I rubbed my hands on my jeans. I was nervous.

I always got butterflies when facing an unknown situation. And unknown situations were the story of my life lately. Every situation was different. Every situation was new.

Rhiannon sat next to the box, which was another

strange thing. Just as she'd insisted on going to Cecilia and Toby's, she'd also insisted on coming home from the shop today. She also smelled different. As if she'd been around someone burning incense, and since I never burned it in the shop, I was wondering what she was getting up to when on her own.

Rhiannon pawed at the box lid.

"What are you trying to tell me, cat?"

She looked at Angelica. The warlock tilted her head and pursed her lips as if thinking.

"What? You're talking to warlocks now, and not me?"

Rhiannon slowly turned her fuzzy black head and speared me with her green eyes.

"All right," I huffed. "Have your conversation. See if I care."

I crossed my arms over my chest and sat back waiting. What can I say? When I'm nervous, I get grumpy. Also, I hadn't had any time alone all summer, let alone enough time with Stefon.

I'd been working my size sixteen butt off with the store, and Stefon had been gone several weekends at his medieval reenactment events. Then I hurt my ankle, and now there was this latest situation to contend with. As per usual, magical emergencies seem to be cropping up left and right, at least once every season.

"When does a witch get a break?" I'm muttered.

"Never," Ah Lam replied. "It is part of the job description."

I uncrossed my arms and sat up, trying to shake off my general nervous, grumpy state.

"So, are you going to let Cyrus and I in on what you two were discussing?"

"Rhiannon is very concerned about this rogue grig.

She feels there may be more than one and wanted to get my take on it."

"And?" I asked, ears perking up. This was interesting.

"I agree. I think there's been far too much damage caused for a single grig. There are either more grigs, or this grig has help."

Like kite guy and Carlson.

"And I know we already all suspected that someone else is in charge," she said.

"Well, that seems obvious," I said, "but who?"

"The million-dollar question," Uncle Cyrus replied, crossing his legs and adjusting his shirt cuffs. I swear, even his summerwear had cuffs, which seemed wacky to me. But then I mostly lived in T-shirts and jeans, didn't I? Who did I have to impress? My customers loved me. My cat tolerated me. And my boyfriend? Well. He liked my jeans just fine. Let's leave it at that.

Rhiannon batted at my arm.

::*Pay attention!*::

Right.

"Unfortunately," I said, dragging my thoughts back to the question at hand, "there's no way to find out before tomorrow, is there?"

"No," said Ms. Wu, tapping her tastefully polished nails against the chair arm. "But it means we have to be on the lookout for several different people. And the teens need to know that, and not just focus on the grig."

Or grigs. I just hoped that grigs actually looked the way they did in Jerry Hamamoto's Faeries' Oracle deck. If not? I guess we'd just look for a fae creature pulling pranks or wreaking havoc.

Cyrus cleared his throat. "Despite your invitation from the runner on the beach, we've already decided that the adults should not attend the party itself, because we'll likely stand out too much."

"Especially you two." I took a sip of my own soda water.

Ah Lam quirked her lips. "Are you calling us old, Sarah?"

I almost spit my water out.

"No! I'm just saying you're too well dressed for a beach rave." I coughed into my elbow and tried to compose myself. "You really think this plan of yours is going to work? With the box and all the rest?"

The warlocks had cooked up some other tricks besides the box the sprites were in, but wouldn't share the information with me. It was one of those annoying need-to-know basis situations.

Well, I guess I'd find out the night of the party, wouldn't I?

Ah Lam leaned forward, the dark sheet of her hair falling around her shoulders. Her eyes were alight with interest, and she was practically rubbing her hands together. All signs of a magical being who loves magical tech.

"Oh yes. The tech is very, very good."

A geek is a geek, whether the tech is silicon chips or magic.

"And you said you had a second crystal ball to link up to Mom's?" The hope was that linking the crystals would enable me to far-see whatever the grig and his friends were doing from a safe distance without having to lug my mother's magical tool around. A crystal orb as big as my head isn't exactly unobtrusive.

Uncle Cyrus nodded, rummaging through the satchel at his feet. He emerged with a beautiful perfect sphere of white quartz clutched in his hand. The crystal had just enough occlusions and striations to catch the light and capture a witch's attention as she tranced.

My mother's box began to hum and rock. Rhiannon batted at the lid again.

"Well, I guess Mom wants in on whatever this is."

It was now or never, and everything pointed to now. So, I took a deep breath, connected with my center, and slowly unlatched the box. Inside, my mother's crystal ball still rang and hummed, but the thumping around had calmed, thank the Goddess.

I withdrew it from its silk and velvet wrappings and grabbed the small, silver-ringed pedestal it sat on. The ball was around the size of a bowling ball and just as beautiful as the smaller version Cyrus held in his long fingers.

"Hello, old friend," I murmured, stroking the smooth, cool surface as I set it on the silver base. I held my hands half an inch away from the surface of the ball, closed my eyes, and concentrated, opening to communication with the magical object. I tried to convey to the crystal what it was we wanted by thinking at it. Really hard.

Next was the cantrip, a witch's rhyme that helped to set spells and other magical workings.

Breathe in. Exhale. I swore that Rhiannon, Cyrus, and Ah Lam all breathed with me. It was nice to feel the support.

"Form a link, a magic chain, join two worlds, and back again. A bond between two crystal spheres, one with me, the other, here."

As the energy built between me and the large crystal ball, Uncle Cyrus leaned forward and held out the smaller orb. He gently placed the crystal in my left hand as I touched the larger with my right.

"Please bridge this gap from far to near."

When the final word of the cantrip was spoken, the smaller crystal in my left hand began to warm, and my hand drifted closer and closer to the large crystal sphere until, *click* the two spheres were touched. They began to hum and vibrate together shaking and moving. I had to really hold on.

"Cyrus?" I asked.

"Just keep breathing," he said.

"And hold on," Ah Lam said. "We will help to settle them."

Both warlocks got to their knees and drew closer to the coffee table, holding out their hands as if to enfold me.

The warlocks poured their energy toward me and Rhiannon began to run zoomies in a circle around us all, faster and faster, raising energy to lend it to the task. I drew upon that wild feline energy, and caught threads from Ah Lam and Cyrus, and wove them all together with my own, tighter and tighter, forming a net that I wrapped around both crystal balls.

"Bind to each other and bind to me to work, together the world to see, until those who are lost are found and free, as I do will, so mote it be!"

With a flash of blinding light and a spark of fire, the magic set itself.

I yelped, but held on, waiting until I could feel the two spheres separate again, the smaller in my left hand. The larger palmed by my right.

I opened my eyes and sat back, cradling the smaller sphere, as Rhiannon leaped up on the couch next to me and began to purr.

I looked from my uncle to Ah Lam Wu.

"Well, I think that worked." Now the small crystal ball would be able to see whatever my mother's crystal would have picked up. It should act like a visual walkie-talkie. Or something.

Ah Lam laughed, and Cyrus smiled.

"I believe it did," he said, "and I believe that means we have earned a glass of wine."

"I need a large glass of water first," I said. "And Rhiannon, how about you?"

::I deserve a treat,:: she said. Now it was my turn to laugh.

"Indeed you do." She allowed me to scratch under her chin. I began to rise, but Cyrus waved me down.

"I'll get everything. It is my wine, after all."

He must have snuck a bottle into my kitchen when I wasn't looking. He's a real snob, that uncle of mine, and whatever alcohol I can afford is never good enough for him.

My snobbery is reserved for tea. Speaking of which...

I called into the kitchen. "Cyrus? What I really want is a large mug of tea."

24

We were on the shallow dunes just above Strawberry Cove, peering down at the beach.

"You know what you're doing right?" I said. Sending the teenagers into this mess made me very nervous.

"Of course, we do," Tabitha said, "we've been over it a thousand times. Besides, Delta made us some clutch amulets." She held up a copper sphere. I could feel traces of magic emanating from it, even from half a yard away.

Tracy patted her friend on the shoulder. "Adults just get nervous."

Wasn't that the truth? Especially adults sending teenagers into danger. Carol stood near me, face tense, gripping her hands.

"Are you sure we shouldn't go in with them?"

"Mom," Tracy said, "if a bunch of adults show up, the party's over before it began."

"Well, we did get an invitation, but they're probably right," I conceded. It wasn't that adults my age wouldn't be welcome, it was that strange—and even queer in my case

—as we were, we looked a bit too straight for this party. Not cool enough anymore.

And oh so not into raves and drugs.

"Hey, Carol," Stefon said, "I get that you're worried, but Rolf and I have all the coms set up. Tracy and Tabitha both have an earbud and Cyrus and Ah Lam are within sprinting distance."

Rolf gave Carol a thumbs-up. I still don't think she was buying it.

"They're keeping the sprites safe," I said. "But they also have more magical backup."

That they hadn't explained to me. I just had to trust, the way Carol did. What I didn't remind people of was that they were closer than sprinting distance. Cyrus could pop in and out as he wished, and so could Ms. Wu. Warlocks. What can I say? Not that I was jealous.

Except of course I was.

"Remember," I said, "look for the grig. And there might be more than one."

"We know, we know." Both teens were quick to reassure me. That would have to be good enough.

"Everyone get in position," I said, as we watched pairs and trios of teenagers and people in their early twenties heading toward the little cave.

"How big is that place, anyway?" I asked.

Stefon shrugged. "Big enough, looks like. Though for all we know, Mr. Magic Fairy Dust dot Com can turn it into a Tardis."

Point taken.

I scanned my brain for my checklist. We had coms. Cyrus and Ms. Wu had tech. The teens both had protective amulets.

I looked out at the ocean and the seagulls calling, the

kite person packing up their wares, and the waves gently caressing the shore. Then I took in a deep, cleansing breath, the way every fake yoga teacher taught you to. But what can I say? That stuff works.

"You okay, babe?"

"Well enough," I said. "Except I wish I was the one going in."

"I know. But we've gone over this." He squeezed my hand.

"I know," I said, squeezing back. Sometimes that's all there was to say. I know didn't feel like enough, but it would have to do for now.

"All right, girls." Carol gave both teens a big hug and kissed Tracy on the side of the temple. "Go get them."

"Okay Mom!"

Both teens trotted off to the pathway, sneakers dangling over their shoulders. We saw them come out the other side, onto the beach, racing and laughing barefoot across the sand. All we could do was watch and hope that nothing bad happened.

My phone buzzed. It was Uncle Cyrus.

We're in position, he had typed. *Ready for anything.*

Teens just went in, I replied, and got a thumbs-up emoji back. I had to admit, it warmed me inside to be working like this with my uncle, even though it meant my parents weren't here to do the job that they had started.

No one ever mentioned the way carrying on a legacy could make you sad.

But if I had to do this work with anyone, Uncle Cyrus was the way to go.

The low *thump thump thump* of music emerged from the cave along with muffled shrieks. It wasn't loud, but definitely noticeable.

"How have they been keeping this from the cops?" I muttered.

"Don't you see that shimmering bubble?" Delta asked, walking up from behind us. She set the tote bag on the ground so that Preston could climb out.

"What bubble?"

The gnome clambered up on a stone bench and peered out towards the cave.

"Clear as day," he said.

My head snapped back towards the cave entrance. Huh? Delta was right. There *was* a bubble. And it hadn't been there five minutes ago.

"They must have just put that up. That means the party is closed now. If you're not inside, or you don't have a flyer, you don't get in."

The teens had researched the website and found a sigil on both the website and the fliers. We'd examined it, and Ah Lam said the sigil was a key into the party.

So, closing the bubble was smart thinking. It meant they could raise a magic bubble, but stragglers could still enter, while ordinary folks would pass on by.

Unfortunately, it was also deadly thinking. Who knows how many people had gotten hurt from the faery dust so far? And how many other sprites had been affected by the thefts?

"What do we do now?" Carol asked. I looked at the worried mother.

"We wait," I said. We all sighed, and settled in.

I sent out a prayer that nothing went terribly wrong.

25

"I really hope they're okay," Carol said. A breeze had whipped up and flung her blond hair across her face, partially shielding her worried expression.

"The amulets should help," I said. "And they're both smart. But will that be enough? Only one way to find out."

Carol shot her head towards me and glared. Oops, not a thing a non-parent should say to a parent.

We were as far away from the cave entrance as we could be, while still being within running distance. Though the jury was still out on that for me. My ankle was good enough to walk on now, thanks to the Babbling Brook, but I hadn't tested jogging yet.

"Hey," a voice called out. "Board Wax!"

Tetris's voice hit me right before the yellow retriever jammed his enthusiastic snout into my crotch.

"Augh!" I said, struggling to fight him off. I swear, the dog needed boundaries. Some friendly is too friendly.

"Board Wax! No!" Tetris jogged towards us, his tattered Crass T-shirt flapping around his skinny body as Stefon, laughing uproariously, tried to pull Board Wax off me.

"I don't blame you, dog," Stefon said. "But it's not polite to do that without consent."

"Very. Funny."

"What?" Stefon replied, grinning, and waggling his eyebrows. "I'm just saying."

I didn't know whether I wanted to kiss his round, bearded face, or whack him. So, I did neither.

"Tetris! I thought you were guarding Carlson."

"I was, but Carlson thought that Board Wax was my ticket in. And Liam agreed and said he and Sophie would keep an eye out."

I shook my head. This was so not according to plan.

"I know. I know," he said, hands waving and Board Wax's leash jingling. "I know what you're thinking. I'm old."

Well, I had been thinking that, but luckily had shut my mouth before the words blurted themselves out. I mean, the old punk rocker was in his fifties, which most people wouldn't consider old, but for the party in the cave? Yeah. Creepy granddad material. Even if he was your cool punk creepy granddad.

He clipped the leash onto Board Wax's collar. The dog whined and tugged before finally lying down.

"So? What do you think?" Tetris asked. His face was slightly flushed from his run. "You think I should try?"

"No," I said.

"Yes," said Carol.

Now we glared at each other, hands on our hips.

"I'd rather have someone we trust in there with them than have them on their own." Her mouth was set.

And Delta, the traitor, was nodding along. Stefon and Rolf backed away. Smart men.

"But if he blows the cover..." I started to say, but Carol cut me off.

"I don't care. I think he's right. It's the perfect cover. Board Wax will be happy to see everyone, and everyone will be happy to see Board Wax."

The dog lifted his head, panting and grinning. He thumped his feathery tail. Clearly Board Wax agreed.

"Just let them try," Stefon said. Guess he wasn't staying out of it after all.

"All right. I'm clearly out-voted. Here," I said, fishing a hand into my back pocket, "take this flier. They won't let you in without it. We think it's a magical key of some sort."

I took in another deep cleansing breath of the ocean air, wiggled my toes in my sneakers, and opened out to the sand, the water, and the sky. Slowing my breathing down, I anchored all the tools in my witch's toolbox with the still center at my core. I felt the smaller crystal ball in my right hand. It began to hum, just like my mother's crystal did.

"Guess we're ready. Hope this works."

I held the ball up and viewed the ocean through its cloudy occlusions, then breathed across the surface, activating it and tuning it further to my magic.

I could See.

I gasped. "It works."

A babble of voices surrounded me.

"What's happening? What do you see?"

Images swirled like a kaleidoscope, finally settling on a group of young people laughing and dancing, arms raised, swaying to music. Pockets of teens giggled uncontrollably, rolling on the sandy floor.

A shimmering dust filled the air, as if someone had taken a load of glitter and thrown it with wild abandon.

That beautiful dust filled me with dread.

There was a grig. At least I assume it was a grig. It looked like a clownfish, if a clownfish had a pale, humanoid face plus arms and legs. In other words, its clothing was really bright. The grig wore a jester's cap and particolored clothing in blue, yellow, and red. It laughed and danced and shook a stick festooned with bells.

But there was something else. Something more sinister, just at the edges of the scene.

I breathed across the surface of the ball again.

"Let me see," I whispered. "Show me what is true."

And there, huddled in the corner of the cave, looking genial and smug, was Buster. He wore a bordering-on-obscene T-shirt with faeries whose breasts were not only impossibly aerodynamic, but larger than mine. And that's saying something.

"Holy moly!"

"What? What is it?" Carol's voice pierced my attention.

"It's Buster! Angie's new baker! No wonder he was poking around at Cecilia and Toby's." It had struck me as odd that Angie would have brought him to help with the delivery. The weasel. "I think he's the one in charge of all of this. Angie said he wanted a raise, but I guess he decided to sell faery dust instead, and rope a bunch of other people into his operation. The greedy git."

Not that Stuart, Carlson, or any of the others were completely blameless, but depending on Buster's powers? They may have been coerced, just like the gargoyles were.

Just then a leering face emerged in the ball, magnified as if the crystal had a fisheye lens.

The grig. And it didn't look nearly as friendly or cheerful as the one on Brian Froud's card.

"Dang it!" I clapped my hand over the crystal ball and shoved it in my pocket. "They're onto us."

"Now what?" asked Rolf.

"Now we hope that Tetris knows what he's doing. And that the magic in the teen's amulets is holding firm."

And since our cover was blown, we might as well go fight.

26

"We have to get down there! Now!" I shouted. "Get Uncle Cyrus and Ms. Wu!"

"Wait! What?" Stefon squawked.

Rolf spoke rapidly into his coms system, but I had no time to waste, and took off running, heading toward the pathway that would lead us to the beach and the little faery-dust-filled cave.

When I got there, the beach was deserted.

Seagulls screamed overhead, and waves crashed. It being August, it was still bright, though the sun was beginning its slow descent toward the horizon. I heard shouts from up ahead mixed with Board Wax, barking frantically.

When I rounded the corner, onto the stretch of beach leading to the cave, my ankle twinged. I stumbled but righted myself. I could hear Stefon running behind me. He would catch up soon. I just hoped he'd been able to alert my uncle in time.

I followed the sound of Board Wax's barking, and the faint thump of music mixed with the high calls of the gulls and the gentle breaking of waves on the shore. The sun was lowering toward the horizon, bathing everything in an orangey salmon light. I tasted salt and brine and something else that I could not place.

"Babe." Stefon was beside me, slowing his jog to match my feeble pace. "Your ankle still okay?"

"It's fine," I said. I really did need to send Uli and the Babbling Brook a gift. Some sort of thank you.

"What's the plan?"

I saw it then, that barely-there bubble of protective magic. A shield so large someone very powerful must have made it. Or a group of powerful people.

"There's a protective sphere around this whole space. I'm not sure I can breach it."

"I'm not sure you should try," Stefon replied, peering at the low sandy hills and the cave. I could tell he was looking for the sphere and not seeing it. "At least, not until backup gets here."

His coms link started squawking.

"Here," he said. "Uh huh. Yeah. Alert Cyrus and Ms. Wu that there's some sort of bubble around this place. We might need backup."

As he was speaking, a multicolored streak raced across the sand, chased by a blond retriever with a feathery tail. Board Wax barked joyfully, as if at play. Tetris and the teens barreled out behind the dog, heels kicking up sand as they ran. The multicolored streak hit the edge of the bubble.

In my mind, I heard a supersonic boom, then a cracking sound as if a giant sheet of ice was split in two.

"Duck!" I yelled, trying to shove my massive boyfriend behind me.

"Sarah?" Stefon bellowed, incredulous that I was

protecting him. Knights. I love 'em, but sometimes they need to stay out of the way.

"Stay back!"

I threw up a shield right as the multicolored blur flung itself into the air, wrapping long, skinny arms around my neck, and long, skinny legs around my hips. Then the thing grabbed my ears like jug handles and held on.

"Woooooooo hoooooooooo!" it shrieked. "Take me for a ride! Take me for a ride! Take me for a ride!"

My shields fell to the sand, completely busted. Need to get quicker on the draw. Dang it!

"Get off me!" I grabbed at the little hands and pulled, but the grig—that's what this thing had to be—held on tighter. Its little face looked like one of those Ren Faire commedia dell'Arte masks. Broad forehead, jutting chin that curled up around leering lips, but instead of the long commedia nose, this one had a tiny pale button.

Made me wonder how it even breathed.

"Not until you take me for a ride. Gotta broomstick, don'cha? Always wanted to fly on a broom. Seems like fun. Are you fun? You don't seem like too much fun. Want some dust? That'll make you fun."

Board Wax danced around us, pawing and barking as if this was all great fun. I swung this way and that, whipping my head around and flinging my torso left and right, trying to dislodge the grig without reinjuring my ankle.

"Aargh! Some help would be nice here! Anytime!"

The grig honked my nose, cackling wildly.

"I'm trying, but the thing has some sort of protection around you both." Stefon sounded winded, as if he'd been sparring in full armor.

"Sarah!" Tracy's voice joined the clamor around me.

"Sarah!" That was Tetris.

"Sarah!" Tabitha.

Why did I have so many friends whose names began with T?

"Get. Me. Cyrus," I grunted out, sending my magical senses out, probing the edges of...dang it. Sure enough, there was a warded sphere around the grig and around me. At least around my upper body.

Aha! If the sphere was only around my upper body, I should be able to reach beyond it. I pushed my energy field deep into the sand, down to where dry sand met wet, and I pulled. Pulled up power from the sand. Power from the ocean. Pulled down power from the sky.

Well, that part didn't work. The power from the sky bounced right off the top of the grig's sphere.

But the power from sand and ocean swept upward in a rush, filling my body, rising, rising, rising.

Then. I. Pushed. Flinging the energy outward, shattering the grig's sphere.

"Stefon! Grab!"

Luckily, he knew what the heck I was talking about, and in seconds, his big hands wrestled the cackling grig off of me.

"Ow!" The grig took a few strands of my hair, gripped in its long fingers, and waved them like a shiny dark wave in the air. Okay. That was more than a few strands. I hoped the thing didn't leave a bald spot.

I'm too young for a bald spot. And too vain.

Now it was Stefon's turn to wrestle with the thing.

Come on, Uncle Cyrus. Show up any time now.

I whipped my head around. The teens were trying to help Stefon, though Board Wax kept getting in the way. Tetris was trying to corral the dog, with no success. It was like a clown car. Flashes of color, and limbs flying everywhere.

Carol stood near the fray, attempting to breach the churning whirlwind.

"Carol!"

She stopped, head snapping toward me, just as Tabitha's arm lashed out.

Carol yelped, leaping backwards.

"What?" she called. "I'm trying to help, here!"

I shook my head. "Leave them to it. It's a distraction! We have to get inside that cave."

Realization dawned on her face, and she nodded. Glad I didn't have to convince her.

But I might need some convincing myself.

The thought of facing a bunch of faery-dust-high humans and a mage powerful enough to repeatedly cast that kind of sphere?

I couldn't do it by myself.

As if they heard me, Delta came huffing across the sand, the gnome clinging to her like a tiny backpack.

The cavalry was arriving.

But I needed the big guns.

"Cyrus!" I shouted to the sunset sky.

"You called?"

Uncle Cyrus stood on the beach, between me and the roiling fray, his dark, shaved head painted with the salmon-orange of sunset, his linen clothing rippling in the breeze. Ah Lam stood just past that, between the heaving tussle and the waves, her dark hair lifting around her head gracefully. How the heck did she do that?

I spat some strands of my own hair out of my mouth, looking from her to the ocean, where the sun rapidly descended to the place where water kissed the sky.

Wait. Sunset.

That felt important, but I wasn't sure how. But I felt in my bones that we were running out of time. Whatever was going to happen, would happen very soon.

The crystal sphere buzzed and chimed inside my pocket.

"Cyrus! We're almost out of time. We need to get inside the cave!"

Ah Lam Wu ran toward me. Uncle Cyrus reached out his arms.

And we were surrounded by music. Strobing lights. Dancing people, arms held high, faces washed with ecstatic joy.

The walls of the cave rose around us, lit from below with multicolored lights that reflected up and off the ceiling. A fog machine pumped out sparkling drifts of shimmering white and gray that billowed through the dancing throng. Just the way I'd seen it in the crystal.

Except the sparkling mist lacked the acrid tang of the fog machines from my Portland clubbing days. And fog didn't shimmer like that.

"Faery dust," I muttered.

"What?" Carol shouted in my ear. I didn't realize Cyrus had transported her as well.

"Faery dust!" I shouted, just as a slice of silence broke between songs. Just my luck, this place had hired a DJ who was terrible at transitions.

My words hung in the air. Heads turned my way.

"What?" a voice said.

Then the *ooncha ooncha ooncha* of a driving techno beat drove the dancers into a frenzy once again.

But walking toward me was Buster. This time, he didn't have a smile and was definitely *not* carrying a freshly baked cinnamon-swirl muffin, which was a pity, because I could use one right about now.

Instead, in his hand was a crystal-tipped wand.

Then he smiled, but not a happy one. The smile looked as if Buster was a shark, and I was a tasty seal.

"Well," Buster said, "if it isn't Sarah, the not-so-teenage witch. What brings you to my little soirée?"

My skin crawled and I was trying hard to not breathe in all the glittering dust floating through the air. I wish we had thought to bring masks.

"Buster. Aren't you a little old for all this?" I gestured around at the dancing youth bouncing up and down, waving their bodies in ecstasy. They were feeling no pain. And that was what this toad of a man was selling.

He laughed. "Never too old to have a good time. But you didn't answer my question."

He reached forward and grabbed my left arm hard enough to bruise.

"What brings you to my little soirée?"

"Hands off," Stefon said.

I swear my boyfriend was practically flexing right there in the middle of everything. I had been so distracted by Buster, I hadn't even seen him arrive.

"How did you get in here?" I asked, but Stefon just shook his head. Right, not now. Another discussion we were going to have later. Along with why he was all of a sudden going all protector dude on me. As if he hadn't seen me take care of myself before.

"I'm fine," I said to him, jerking my arm from Buster's meaty grasp. "Find Tracy and Tabitha."

We really needed to make sure the teens were okay, and I couldn't be in two places at once.

"That's right, little man. Run along, Stefon." Buster drawled Stefon's name. Stefon growled. I don't know why my boyfriend was so insulted. He was the larger of the two, and could probably snap Buster like a twig, even though Buster wasn't exactly small himself.

Come to think of it, neither am I.

"Stefon."

He gave Buster one last glower and faded into the roiling crowd. I turned back to the smirking baker, still wondering what the heck kind of magic he wielded. It had to be strong.

"I came here because you're causing trouble in my town. Stealing from the fae. Feeding humans drugs. Why, Buster? Baking not enough? Do you really need the money that badly?"

He laughed again, his belly shaking like Old King Cole's.

"*Your* town? My, my, my. You don't have self-esteem issues, do you?"

"I don't. As a matter of fact," I said straightening my shoulders and planting my feet more firmly in the sand, "that should worry you."

"Why is that?" He still sounded smug, but something flashed across his eyes. I couldn't tell if it was worry or something else.

"Because we're going to take you down," said Ah Lam, appearing beside me.

And then all hell broke loose.

28

The DJ switched to a new song. A roar swept through the crowd, and people seemed to shout and dance even harder than before. I couldn't tell you what the song was, because, well, I don't keep up with the latest club hits anymore.

Buster reached out and grabbed my throat. I inhaled sharply, taking in a huge draught of faery-dust-laden air. My eyes widened, and I coughed it right back out into his face.

"Augh! You!" he bellowed, easing up on my throat enough for me to break his grip by grabbing his thumbs and pulling them outward.

"Aauuugghh!" he bellowed again.

"Let go!" I shoved him backwards, but he reached for me again. I could hear Board Wax barking and suddenly, Rhiannon was there, spitting and yelling and climbing Buster's head and shoulders.

"What the heck? Rhiannon!"

::*Not now!*:: she shouted. ::*Get the grig!*::

"What?"

::The grig!::

Rhiannon snarled and lashed out at the still-flailing Buster.

You have to trust, Sarah. A voice sounded in my head. I recognized it as my own witchy wisdom. Whenever that voice speaks, I always listen.

I raced through the crowded cave, shoving through dancing bodies and trying not to think about all the sweat, and faery dust, and who knew what else was flying through the air.

I followed the sound of Board Wax's barking, and found the dog, Tetris, Tabitha, and Tracy all fighting with the grig. The creature bounced like a multicolored maniac, jumping from person to person, cackling with glee. The grig flung still more glittering dust into the air from a pouch he clutched in one hand.

"Where's your mother?" I shouted to Tracy.

"I don't know!" she shouted back, reaching for the grig's arm and missing. "Help us!"

I looked around to see if there was any backup to be had, but Cyrus and Ah Lam were in one corner of the cave, huddled over what looked like a strange steampunk machine. Those two had more gadgets than I'd ever imagined were possible. Must be nice working for the council. But at any rate, they weren't going to be any help. Though where was Stefon?

"Sarah! Help!" The grig had latched onto Tabitha's back and was riding her like she was a centaur.

Right. It was up to me.

I took a deep breath, drawing on the power of the sand beneath my sneakers, and felt the magic roll through me and pour out my hands. When it reached my fingertips, I lashed out and grasped the grig by its multicolored colored tunic, slamming its back into my chest. It started to whoop and tried to turn and grab at me, but I pinioned its arms.

The thing struggled against me, and battered its legs against my thighs, but the spindly limbs were no match for my strong, well-padded body.

"Where did you get the faery dust?" I yelled into the closest ear.

"Nyah, nyah nyah! Not telling!"

I squeezed tighter.

"Where did you get the faery dust?" I repeated.

"Not. Telling." The grig was wheezing now but showing no signs of letting go. It had managed to squirm and turn itself halfway toward me. I so did not want to be anywhere near its mouth. Whether grigs bit or not, I didn't know. And I didn't want to find out.

I squeezed harder. Its sneering commedia dell'arte face was turning red.

"Where did you get the faery dust!" I was screaming now, partly because of the noise in the cave, and partly out of frustration.

"I stole it."

"Why?" Tracy shouted.

"Looked like fun! Why should the sprites hoard all that? Besides, Buster paid me!"

"You have got to be kidding me," I said. "You stole the sprites' faery dust because you wanted to party? And why do grigs need money?"

"Of course I wanted to party! Who wouldn't? Except an old stick-in-the-mud like you. Buster understood. Buster's a witch too. But Buster knows how to have fun. And Buster pays in things I like. Shining things. Pretty things. Yummy things."

Board Wax barked.

Buster the faery dust dealer was going to get what was coming to him, that was for sure. But right now, I needed to immobilize the grig so it couldn't do any more damage. And then I needed to get back to Buster, hoping he hadn't killed my cat.

And where was Stefon?

"Tetris!" I shouted over the *ooncha ooncha* of the music, and cries of "whoop, whoop!" from the crowd.

"What?" Tetris leaned closer.

"Do you have Board Wax's leash?" I hadn't seen it in the cave, but that didn't mean that Tetris didn't have one squirreled away somewhere. I hoped.

He shook his head mournfully. "Got lost."

"Use my belt!" Carol said.

The motley-colored grig squirmed in my arms, struggling. An elbow jammed into my left breast.

"Ouch! Hold still!"

"Not while you imprison me!" it cried. "A grig must live free or die! I will not be chained or detained!"

Tetris shoved a handkerchief in the grig's mouth. "That's enough, you."

Carol was there with her belt, and between the three of us, we got the belt tied firmly around the grig's flailing arms. That just left his legs, which I didn't think of until he kneed me in the kidney.

"Anyone else have a belt?"

Tabitha whipped a leather belt festooned with flat-head studs from around her size four hips and the two teens secured the thrashing grig's legs. Right about then, Stefon showed up from who knows where.

"You aren't helping Rhiannon?" I screeched. What can

I say, sometimes when I'm startled or upset, my voice rises an octave or three.

He grinned. "Rhiannon is fine. You'll see. Besides, Cyrus and Ah Lam sent me over to secure this little guy."

"Mmmrph! Muumph!" The grig wiggled like a fish on a dock, but the leather belts held. Good.

"Can you sit on him or something? We need to keep him secure."

I didn't care what my knightly boyfriend said about Rhiannon. I had to make certain she was safe.

"I can do you one better. Cyrus magicked in some kind of secure box. Says its ventilated for transport."

The grig thrashed harder. Even with its arms and legs bound, I still struggled to hold on.

"Mmph! Mmm-mmph!" The grig's thrashing increased, making it harder and harder to hold on.

"Can you take him?"

"Sure babe."

Suddenly, my arms were empty, and my boyfriend was slipping through the crowd like someone a third of his size.

And Tetris and the teens were gone.

29

My eyes burned from the glittering air, and I was starting to feel a bit, you know, happy. Everyone around me shrieked with laughter and danced nonstop as if they wore the proverbial red shoes.

"This isn't right," I muttered, but I said it with a smile on my face. I was grinning so hard it felt like my face would crack any second. I needed to find my friends, and we needed to stop this party before someone else got hurt.

"Hey, pretty lady! Dance with us!"

I was surrounded by a joyous, bouncing group, and found myself bouncing, too. I knew it wasn't right. I had a cat to save and sprites to protect and I just didn't care.

This moment was all that mattered. The music. The dancing. The sheer joy of it. I was buoyed by the crowd, and the taste of faery dust and salty sea air.

This is what the grig was talking about. I got it now.

The grig.

It was as if a record scratched inside my head, marring the music. Bringing the moment to a halt.

At least, it did inside of me. Everyone else was still

having a grand old time. The party girl and the responsible Justice warred inside of me. The Justice part won. Barely.

I smiled and bounced my way out of the circle, threading through the crowd. It really was easier to navigate the space while dancing. Note to self in case I ever came across a faery--dust imbibing group of people again.

Which I hoped was not likely.

Finally, I saw Board Wax dancing excitedly around Buster, barking his fool head off. Rhiannon still clung to Buster's back, yowling and hanging on for dear life as Tabitha, Tracy, and Tetris—the latter laughing hysterically—all tried to get close enough to Buster to help her.

Just then, Preston the gnome vaulted onto the top of Buster's head, kicking his face with tiny, booted feet, as Board Wax raced around Buster's legs.

"Sarah!" Delta shouted in my ear. "Snap out of it! You have to stop this!"

I looked down at Delta, whose gray hair stuck out in wild tufts all around her head. She looked furious.

"How is the faery dust not affecting you?" The more I tried to stop grinning, the harder it became.

"Because I am a witch who knows how to ward herself!" she huffed, then started sketching symbols in the air around my head.

"I did ward…"

With a loud *pop*, my head cleared, and I could breathe properly again.

"Oh." I took in a full body breath. Maybe I hadn't warded properly after all. No time to think about it now.

I scanned for my witch's tools. Felt the crystal orb in my pocket. What else could I use? Athame? Cup? No. Wand. I needed my wand. I reached out and sent a thought to the altar in my bedroom. Imagined the smoothness of oiled hawthorn wood. The shape that perfectly fit my hands.

Then I pulled, and my wand was in my left hand. I pointed it at Buster, trying to find a space between Preston's arms and legs and the perpetual motion machine that was Rhiannon and her murder claws.

Dang it! It wasn't going to work. I needed a clear shot.

"Count of three!" I shouted, both out loud and with my mind. Preston's head whipped toward me, and Rhiannon's eyes grew wide.

"One!"

Cat and gnome both scrabbled for purchase on Buster's bleeding head and shoulders.

"Two!"

Tabitha and Tracy both held out their arms.

"Three!"

Cat and gnome both leapt, caught by the teens, right as a blast from my wand hit Buster squarely on the nose, knocking him down.

Board Wax stood on the downed baker, four paws planted firmly on his chest and stomach, licking Buster's face.

"Smells like cinnamon, doesn't he, boy?" Tetris asked, giving Board Wax a pat on the head. Then he yanked at the cables snaking their way to the DJ booth. The sound cut off with a squawk, leaving the air filled only with the sound of Buster moaning, and all the faery-dust-stoned people still laughing and dancing, as if nothing much had changed.

Tetris made short work of binding Buster with the cords and cables.

And the sound of a massive vacuum filled the air.

30

Ah Lam held a giant vacuum nozzle with both hands, waving it through the air, sucking down the sparkling dust as Uncle Cyrus worked the steampunk-looking controls. The snaking vacuum was connected to yet another box—how many boxes did those two bring?—which I assumed was some faery dust retrieval and storage system.

All I knew was that the air grew clearer every second. People began dropping to the sandy cave floor, maniacal laughter turning to soft giggles. I breathed a sigh of relief. These people, at least, seemed as if they'd be okay.

I looked around. Tabitha still held Rhiannon—who looked pretty dang pleased with herself—and Tracy held Preston. Good. Then Carol, Stefon, and Delta all gathered around. There were a few threads to tie up about this case, but one main thing bothered me.

"Rhiannon?" I asked. "How did you get here?"

::*I teleported.*:: She licked a paw, as if that was that.

I quirked an eyebrow, waiting for more.

::*I enrolled in Magic Cat School.*::

"Magic Cat School?"

Everyone looked confused at that, but Rhiannon turned away. We were so going to be talking about this later.

But meanwhile, I was getting a headache and still had work to do. The sound of the vacuum was annoyingly loud, making it hard to think, but it was doing such a great job of clearing the air, I suppose I shouldn't complain.

"What now?" Tabitha asked.

I looked down at Buster. His bosomy, scantily clad–faery T-shirt was shredded, and deep scratches scored his face, and a tiny boot print left a dent in his left cheek. That was going to hurt.

But forgive me if I wasn't feeling too sympathetic.

"Now we sentence this clown car," I replied.

The vacuum blessedly stopped roaring and sucking up faery dust. Uncle Cyrus must have flipped the switch.

I took a moment to compose myself, to reconnect to my center. Switching my wand to my right hand, I took a deep breath. It smelled of clean, salt air and nothing else.

Settling into my body and opening my heart and mind, I reached for my witch's intuition and the power I held as named Justice. The magic winged its way toward me, filling me from head to toe.

"Buster! The powers that be bind you from causing further harm. You may no longer lie, steal, use magical creatures as drug mules, or wear tacky T-shirts!"

Buster groaned at my feet. Okay. That last part was a little mean, but the guy deserved it.

"To make amends to the sprites, the gargoyles, and all these people, I sentence you to build a garden and tend bees in the abandoned lot at the edge of town."

I happened to know the Seashell Cove beautification

committee had been talking about just that scheme and would welcome a major volunteer.

"The sprites and other small magical creatures are allowed free access to the space at any time. And to make amends to all the people you have drugged, or put in the hospital, or disappeared? You are to donate any profits from your parties to their care if they should want or need it. And that's gross. Not net."

Buster struggled to sit up, which was hard, considering how thoroughly Tetris had tied him. Stefon and Tetris both helped him into an upright position. He looked at me, eyes pleading, as Board Wax pawed my leg.

I looked down at the golden lab, whose tongue lolled from his head.

"Yes, Board Wax?"

He barked, three times.

::Rhiannon, do you know what Board Wax is saying?::

::Dogs don't always speak so clearly. Let's see. Something, something, Fun Run.:: she replied.

Of course!

I held the wand steady as I concluded my sentencing.

"And any remaining money goes to the Wag a Lot Fun Run to support the Seashell Cove animal shelter."

Buster burst into tears, head hanging to his chest.

"Do you agree to this sentence?"

"Do I have a choice?" he sobbed.

"No."

"Then I do."

"Buster, with the powers of magic, and the powers of Justice, and the powers of this community behind me, I bind you to this task, from this day and for nine years hence."

Board Wax barked again.

"What is it now, good boy?" The dog, who had started out as a major pain, had really ended up being a good boy after all.

::*He wants you to take him for a run,*:: Rhiannon commented.

"He wants me to take him for a run?"

All my friends burst into laughter.

I scowled at first, but then couldn't help it.

I laughed, too. Whether it was the aftereffects of faery dust or not, I didn't care.

Laughing just felt good.

31

I t was a glorious Sunday for the Wag a Lot Fun Run. I'd left Duncan in charge of The Widening Gyre. He had the task of taking care of customers and getting the two gargoyles settled. The stone creatures had decided the bookshop was a dandy place to be, and last I saw them, were busy choosing their favorite spots, perched on the tops of bookshelves, able to watch the whole store.

It wasn't a castle in Scotland, but they seemed to be content with the arrangement, which I hoped would be a boon for the shop. It meant we now had a gargoyle security system. I hadn't banked on that.

Everyone else had the day off, me included. We needed it after the big battle in the cave. Besides, with everyone down at the beach for the start of the run, business should be sparse anyway. I'd spent the past hour giving out dog treats and was ready for the brief run with Board Wax, as promised. I'd offered to let Tetris do the run instead, but the middle-aged punk insisted that he couldn't run in Doc Marten boots.

Fair enough. I missed running anyway.

The sun was shining, but it wasn't too hot. Pennants waved in the breeze, children ran around joyfully, and dogs scampered and played, all excited to be romping in the sand, waiting for the 1K Pet and Human Fun Run to start. The festive swarm was a sight to behold. There were tutus and banana costumes, faery wings and glitter wands. People prepared to run with dogs on the leash and other animals in slings or backpacks. One year there was a duck on a leash, but a dog got a bit too close for comfort, so I guess the duck didn't return.

I had asked Rhiannon if she wanted to run with me in a special cat-pack and she threatened my favorite pair of jeans with grievous harm. So, I took that as a no. Instead, Rhiannon was helping to mind the shop, as usual. She had also said, I quote, *I've had enough sand between my toe beans for this lifetime, thank you. Besides, who will keep an eye on Duncan?*

I decided discretion was the better part of valor and said nothing. It's best to let Rhiannon think she's the boss.

And maybe she is.

"You sure you're ready for this, babe?" Stefon asked as I stretched my hamstrings.

I wiggled my toes in their barefoot-style running shoes, and inhaled the scent of brine, cotton candy, and hot pretzels. Brightly colored kites flapped overhead. The seller we'd met from one beach up had taken over Stuart's spot temporarily, as he recovered. Turned out he'd gotten into a fight with Buster after he figured out that Buster was inviting under age people to the parties where the Happy Dust would be flowing freely.

Buster had pulled a magical whammy on the kite seller, plus thrown the damaging punches and kicks that had sent Stuart to the hospital. I wish I'd known...but that was how these cases worked, wasn't it?

At any rate, I'd heard that Stuart was working out a co-sharing deal with the other kite vendor, which was a nice outcome for all.

Gazing up at the top of the cliffs, where the five- and ten-kilometer runs would start, I nodded.

"I couldn't risk anything longer, but less than a mile?" I replied, as I rotated my ankle. No twinges. "I think I'm good for that. Besides, I made a promise."

As if he heard me, Board Wax came bounding up, panting happily, golden tail waving in the breeze. He was followed by Tetris holding a purple leash, plus Tracy, Tabitha, Carol, Delta, and Preston.

Toby and Cecilia were with my Uncle Cyrus and Ah Lam, helping the sprites. They had vacuumed up enough faery dust to last the local sprites for years. Once the sprites were fully recovered from their ordeal, there was talk of hammering out a plan to get the rest of the faery dust to other sprite colonies up and down the coast.

A voice came over the loudspeaker.

"The Fun Run will begin in ten minutes! Please pin your numbers to your costumes."

My number was already safety pinned to the back of my Biff the Ghost T-shirt, so I was ready. Tabitha and Tracy were crouched down, petting Board Wax, who looked at them with adoring eyes. I was glad the dog had a place to stay, and friends to care for him, because Carlson still seemed a bit shell-shocked. I had wondered about sentencing the surfer, but decided he was a victim of circumstance more than anything else. Besides, Liam said Carlson had turned out to be quite handy and could live at The Historic Kelpie for as long as he liked. So, it felt best to leave well enough alone.

Sometimes that is justice enough.

"Hey!" Tabitha asked, "How come you don't have a costume to run in?"

I gestured to my leggings and T-shirt. "This is my costume."

"I don't get it." She wrinkled her nose. Everyone looked puzzled.

I smiled at my friends.

"I'm going as a witch."

WHAT'S NEXT?

T. THORN COYLE
AUTHOR OF THE WITCHES OF PORTLAND
HALLOWS WITCH
A SEASHELL COVE
PARANORMAL MYSTERY

When a witch gets a warning...
My name is Sarah Braxton, and I'm a witch. It's heading on toward Samhain—Halloween for you civilians out there—and there's another mystery afoot. Someone is leaving dead rats on doorsteps, with a warning painted in blood. Yuck.

It's going to take the whole gang to figure this one out, and my cat Rhiannon is in the thick of things...

Find out what happens in Samhain Witch.

AND MORE...

If you enjoyed this book, please consider telling a friend, or leaving a short review at your favorite booksellers or on GoodReads.
Many thanks!

And visit thorncoyle.com to sign up for a weekly newsletter.

ACKNOWLEDGMENTS

Thank you to Chris and Bonnie for checking my cozy levels early in the process! Thanks to Leslie and Jack for reading, to Dayle for editing, and to my family for years of support.

Most of all, thank you to everyone who fell in love with a witch, a cat, and their wacky friends in a not-so-sleepy seaside town.

ALSO BY T. THORN COYLE

FICTION

Seashell Cove Paranormal Cozy Mysteries

Bookshop Witch

Haunted Witch

Tarot Witch

Running Witch

Hallows Witch

Solstice Witch

The Pride Street Paranormal Cozy Mysteries

Sushi Scandal

Flower Frenzy

Muffin Murder

Hairspray Horror

The Witches of Portland (complete)

By Earth

By Flame

By Wind

By Sea

By Moon

By Sun

By Dusk

By Dark

By Witch's Mark

The Panther Chronicles (Complete)

To Raise a Clenched Fist to the Sky

To Wrest Our Bodies From the Fire

To Drown This Fury in the Sea

To Stand With Power on This Ground

The Steel Clan Saga

We Seek No Kings

We Heed No Laws

We Ride at Night

Short Story Collections

A Hint of Faery

A Touch of Faery

A Spark of Magic

A Flame for Yuletide

A Hope for Winter

A Time for Magic

A Speculation of Stars

A Speculation of Hope

A Speculation of Time

Risk It All: Queer Stories of Love, Suspense, And Daring

Thresholds: Queer Stories of Love, Suspense, And Daring

Cats and Other Creatures

NON-FICTION

Evolutionary Witchcraft

Kissing the Limitless

Make Magic of Your Life

Sigil Magic for Writers, Artists & Other Creatives

Crafting a Daily Practice

Resistance Matters

ABOUT THE AUTHOR

T. Thorn Coyle worked in many strange and diverse occupations before settling in to write books full time. Buy them a cup of tea and perhaps they'll tell you about it.

Author of the *Seashell Cove Paranormal Mystery* series, *The Steel Clan Saga*, *The Witches of Portland*, and *The Panther Chronicles*, Thorn's multiple non-fiction books include *Sigil Magic for Writers, Artists & Other Creatives*, and *Evolutionary Witchcraft*.

Thorn's work appears in many anthologies, magazines, and collections. They have taught magical practice in nine countries, on four continents, and in twenty-five states.

An interloper to the Pacific Northwest U.S., Thorn stalks city streets and talks to crows, squirrels, and trees.

Connect with Thorn:
www.thorncoyle.com